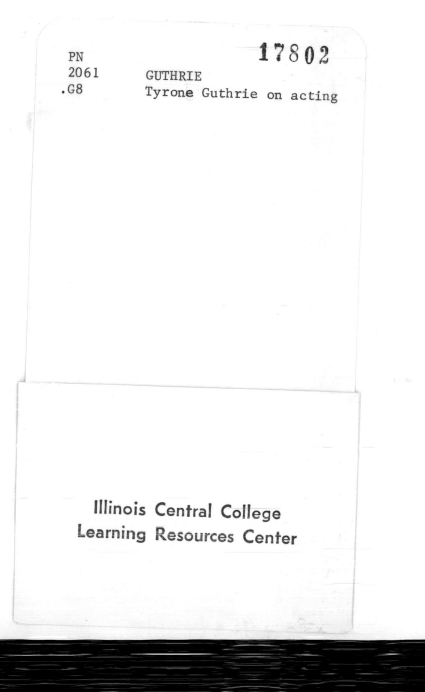

Tyrone Guthrie on Acting

# Tyrone Guthrie on Acting

A Studio Book

The Viking Press · New York

# Acknowledgements

Acknowledgements are due to Zoë Dominic for plates 37, 40–1; to Mark Hanau for plate 27; to the Gabrielle Enthoven Collection at the Victoria and Albert Museum and Peter Hirst-Smith for plates 1–7; to Douglas H. Jeffrey for plates 29, 31–5, 38–9; to John Kobal for plate 17; to Angus McBean for plates 19, 22; to the Raymond Mander and Joe Mitchenson Theatre Collection for plates 8–16, 18, 25; to Sir Laurence Olivier for plates 20–1; to Douglas Spillane for plate 30; to John Vickers for plates 23–4, 26, 28; to Jim Wilson for plate 36.

The design on the front of the jacket is based
on the plan of the auditorium of the Tyrone Guthrie
Theatre at Minneapolis.
The illustration on the back of the jacket is
of Christopher Plummer as Cyrano de Bergerac
at the Stratford Shakespearean Festival Theatre,
Ontario, Canada.

Copyright © Tyrone Guthrie 1971
All rights reserved
First published in Great Britain 1971
by Studio Vista Limited, Blue Star House,
Highgate Hill, London N19
and in the United States of America 1971 by
The Viking Press, Inc.
625 Madison Avenue, New York, NY 10022
Library of Congress Catalog Card Number: 72–150358
Set in 12 pt Bembo
Text printed and book bound in Great Britain
by Richard Clay (The Chaucer Press) Ltd.
Bungay, Suffolk
Illustrations printed in Great Britain by
Fletcher & Son Ltd, Norwich
House editor Anne Kilborn
Designer Ian Craig

American SBN 670–73832–8
British SBN 289 70085 X

# Contents

# 1 *Art and craft*

*What is acting?*

By definition Acting is no more than Doing, Taking Action. But in a specialized sense, the term Acting is used for the Art or Craft of Acting. This implies pretending to be someone or something other than yourself; or even, while retaining your own identity, expressing thoughts or feelings which do not in fact correspond with your own thoughts and feelings at a particular moment. Indeed in this sense of the word we all spend a great deal of our lives in acting, a greater part, I suspect, than most of us realize. Most of it is done in a good-natured endeavour to lubricate the creaking mechanism of social intercourse. This is particularly the case in business or professional dealings. Employees have to make a show to employers of being industrious and respectful, while employers have to make a show of being kind and just and taking an interest. 'How's *Mrs* Wetherbee? . . . Oh, not *again* (in a tone of extreme concern) . . . that's her second this winter.' (With even deeper concern) '*Has* she tried those sort of inhaler things?' Fortunately at this moment the telephone rings and the actor can switch from the rôle of Considerate Employer to that of Jolly Fellow-Rotarian and by the time the 'kidding' and the roars of assumed laughter have run their dreadful course, old Wetherbee, thank God, has slipped out of your office and Miss Scales is ready to take dictation. Whereupon yet another Act begins: the iron-clad, ice-cold Man of Affairs creating order and profit out of chaos; and, at the self-same time, yet another impersonation: the dominant Male allowing a Female to help him, so far as such a flighty, fluffy little thing can be a help in business.

Is this kind of hypocrisy really acting? I think so, because, though you are not pretending to an identity or appearance other than your own, and though you are inventing your own dialogue and choreography, you are, nevertheless, expressing many different facets of your-self, and this, I believe, means that from time to time you are forced, if the facets are to be convincingly displayed, to think of yourself as many different kinds of people, similar only because they all look like you, wear your clothes, speak in your voice and are limited by your, admittedly considerable, limitations.

Yet isn't it possible that most of us are not quite so severely limited as we suppose, and that this sort of acting, which can also be called social adaptability, is a considerable help in expanding our limitations? Incidentally, most of us perform these tricks of adaptability so habitually that we are hardly conscious of them as not being our absolutely 'natural' behaviour.

Of course, practically no social behaviour is 'natural'. It is natural to rush and grab what we want like a baby or an untrained animal; it is natural to growl and scream when our desire is thwarted, be it for a bone, a rattle or a bishopric. Socially acceptable behaviour is a highly unnatural performance, only attainable after considerable training. I sometimes think that if professional actors reflected a little more on how we all learn acceptable social manners, it would be a valuable guide to many of the techniques of their craft.

To return to the definition of acting: in general we use the word to signify pretending to be somebody else in the particular context of drama, a character in a play, of which the theme, the sequence of events (or plot), the nature of the persons and the very words which they speak have all been previously conceived by an author, then written down, then rehearsed (or repeated over and over) by actors. And even this more artificial kind of acting bears a resemblance to the less conscious pretences of social life: the success of the performance depends upon being 'convincing'. In the one case your cheery 'Good morning' must convince Mrs Arbuthnot that you sincerely wish her well. In the other case you must convince an audience, even many successive audiences, that your Hamlet is sufficiently interesting to justify the considerable effort which is demanded of them at this particular play. You must also convince an audience that your assumption is plausible in the given circumstances; that a person, who looks and sounds as you do in the part, might have said the words, felt the sentiments, done the deeds which the author has indicated.

Emphatically this is not the same thing as convincing an audience that you actually are Hamlet. Quite obviously you are not. The intention of the actor should never be to try to deceive the audience into confusing fiction with fact. He should, rather, go through the *ritual* of performance in such a manner as to make the fiction acceptable – not as fact, but as an interesting and pleasurable experience.


*How to make acting plausible*

How does an actor set out to make his performance plausible?

First, by imagination. To impersonate a character successfully you must imagine what it would feel like to *be* that character, how he would move, what his voice would be like, why he says and does whatever he says and does in the play. Of course he says and does these things because he is a person of a certain character, and characters are conditioned partly by their heredity, partly by their environment. Therefore acquaintance with the character whom you are to play involves having a point of view about that character's heredity and environment. Put another way, the actor's study of his rôle must be based first on the factual evidence of the text: what the character reveals about himself and what other people in the play reveal about him. Sometimes there may be good reason to suspect the truthfulness of other people. (In *Hamlet*, for instance, in the soliloquies Hamlet is giving the audience his own perfectly frank point of view and Horatio's evidence about Hamlet is apt to be very reliable. The evidence, however, of Claudius or Polonius is more suspect, for both are repeatedly exposed to the audience as untrustworthy. Consequently, when, for instance, they assert that Hamlet is mad, we do not necessarily believe that Hamlet is in fact mad, especially since Claudius and Polonius both have interested motives in saying so.)

Next the actor must draw deductions from the *actions* of the character he is to impersonate. The statement that Hamlet is mad must be weighed against whether Hamlet does indeed behave like a madman or merely as a man pretending to be mad. His actions now and then are wild enough, but is it a pretended wildness? The extreme lucidity of his reasoning throughout the play does not suggest mental disorder. Again, the widely-held critical theory that he is irresolute does not easily square with the events of the play – the murder of Polonius, for example, the execution of Rosencrantz and Guildenstern, his own dealings with the pirates, to say nothing of his break with Ophelia, which may suggest madness or extreme nervous pressure, but is absolutely not irresolute.

Therefore, in determining how he will play his part, the serious actor must do a great deal of preliminary work, putting himself into this or that imaginary situation, not only those expressed in the text, but others deducible from the text. For instance, how did Hamlet's father feel about his son's career at Wittenberg? Was Uncle Claudius the first to express disapproval? On the evidence of the text, was Hamlet really fond of his father or only afraid of him? How account for his mature, sophisticated advice to the players, spoken 'off the cuff' to people much older than himself? Is it not more than the gracious condescension of a well-informed princely amateur? One cannot quite imagine the Prince of Wales in the green-room before a Command Performance at Windsor Castle thus addressing Mr and Mrs Lunt and Bob Hope.

All this preliminary and largely psychoanalytic work must, in the case of so famous and complex a rôle as Hamlet, be based on extensive reading, comparison of the writings of critics and scholars, discussion with colleagues, director, older actors who have played the rôle, and so on. If, however, you are called upon to play only a small part, Francisco, for example, or the second Gravedigger, the preparatory imagining will be easier and take less time.

But, whether the part be long or short, complex or simple, the actor will, sooner or later, have to translate imagination into practice, theory into action, and to this end it will not come amiss if he has paid some attention not only to *what* is to be expressed and *why* but also *how*. Here he will, inevitably, have to pay some attention to what is called theatrical technique.

*Imagination and technique*

It should be remembered that the division of an actor's work into two compartments, Imagination and Technique, is merely a matter of logical convenience. In fact the two compartments should not, indeed cannot, be kept entirely separate. They overlap and interlock at every stage and in every aspect of the preparation of a play. In the previous paragraph I may have given the impression that thinking and imagination come first, preceding in time the technical matters of giving breath and body to previously conceived ideas. If so, this was simply for the sake of convenience, of trying to be clear and at the same time brief.

With beginners the imaginative process probably does come first, because beginners are as capable of imaginative effort as are veterans and because beginners do not have the veteran's technical accomplishment. They have to learn, almost entirely by experience and at the expense of themselves and the public, how to use their physical equipment: when to move, when to keep still, when to speak slowly and emphatically, when fast and lightly – and not only when but also, harder to learn, how.

Ideally an imaginative intuition should be inseparable from the physical means of its expression. With the most gifted players this is almost always so. But now and again it happens that even the greatest actor will imagine an idea but be unable immediately to find a physical means to express it. He may have to experiment with different emphases, different vocal colours, different inflexions or different movements before he finds the right one. Or, vice versa, he may feel impelled to turn his head, to move his eyes, to breathe more quickly or deeply without immediately knowing why. In general, however, the more gifted the actor, the more completely will his ideas be co-ordinated with the physical means of their expression, and this without the slightest consciousness of such co-ordination. It is the ham who thinks: 'At this point I show anger. Therefore I shout, I stamp, I dilate the nostrils, I clench and unclench the fist.' The truly gifted actor will just feel angry and the technical expressions will occur automatically and in a far less stereotyped manner than those of the ham.

While from time to time imagination may seem to be in one compartment and technique in another, this is an almost entirely artificial distinction. It must be made by teachers and critics and theorists, and by actors, when they are considering the craft which underlies their art. But in the practice of their art they should seek the most complete and unconscious synthesis of theory with practice, imagination with technique.

A logical distinction between imagination and technique and a hoped-for synthesis between the two, exists in all the arts, indeed in all human activity. For instance, the pianist or violinist does not 'put in the expression' by means of solely technical effects. His performance is a mixture of planned form and prearranged effect (analogous to the actor's intellectual and imaginative preparation) with emotional and instinctive reaction to this or that particular occasion. The writer can theoretically distinguish between form and matter, and in the practice of a good writer they are completely interlocked; the one neither precedes nor dominates the other. Indeed one of the measures of the quality of a writer is the degree to which he has achieved the synthesis of form and matter. A great military leader or business administrator or lawyer, doctor or priest is so, in so far as he can unconsciously synthesize theory and practice, form and matter, imagination and technique.

# 2 Different kinds of acting

## Good and bad

Good acting demands that you are 'convincing' in your part. The audience must be willing to take part in a *ritual*, in which you represent, say, Hamlet. You must be able to sustain this representation 'convincingly': that is to say, you must consistently satisfy the audience's imagination and never outrage its acceptance of the fact that yours is a 'convincing', or consistently credible, Hamlet, Mrs Tanqueray or whatever character you are impersonating.

Now, if you want to make someone believe something, there must be at least some correspondence between the impression which you make and the preconception of your auditor. At a very elementary level, if you say, even to so co-operative an audience as a small child, who is not merely willing but eager to suspend disbelief . . . if you say to him: 'I am a bear and I am going to eat you for my supper', the performance will fall pretty flat if your tone and demeanour are implausible. This does not mean that you must literally imitate a bear's growl and put on a bearskin. That would probably scare your audience into a fit. Your voice and demeanour, however, must, to some limited degree, suggest qualities which your audience will recognize as appropriate to the idea of a bear.

At a less elementary level, if the part of Hamlet is to be convincingly played, the actor must make his auditors believe that his Hamlet has at least some clear connection with their preconception. If they have listened carefully to the first scene of the play, they will have heard that Hamlet is a prince, is young and the heir to a troubled kingdom. So an elderly and vulgar actor will have difficulty in being accepted. But literate people come to *Hamlet* with many, many preconceptions, derived from all sorts of sources. Many of these it is almost the actor's duty NOT to embody; but many of them he cannot avoid. To play Hamlet you must be not only adequately youthful and princely, you must deliver the rhetoric with musicianly appreciation and skill, the passion must be credibly passionate, the wit witty, the grief grievous. The audience must be able to accept that, at every single moment of that gigantically demanding impersonation, your words, gestures, what you seem to be thinking and feeling sufficiently correspond with what the text is telling them about Hamlet and with the preconceptions which they have formed. Performance and preconceptions must correspond sufficiently but not necessarily fully: first, no two people's preconceptions are identical and no one's preconception is very detailed or complete. Second, most audiences are willing to take part in the theatre's make-believe (in Coleridge's 'willing suspension of disbelief') to the extent that they will go half-way to meet the actor, will accept him as a prince unless his lack of princely qualities is acute. The point is that the actor need not completely fulfil the demands of his part; he simply must not fall too short.

Clearly it is harder to meet the demands of parts like Hamlet or King Oedipus, which cover immense ranges of feeling and thought, than those of little parts where you are not called upon to do more than come on and say, 'Tennis, anyone?' But even here you must be able to swing your racket convincingly and when, a little later, your rôle expands to, 'I say, Monica, you look divine in blue,' you must eye Monica as though she really were divine. More than that, you must suggest that you too are divine, since in this, and ten thousand similar light comedies, you and Monica supply what is called the Love Interest. You must maintain the audience's belief not only in your own impersonation but in the whole goings-on of which you are but one part. To be 'convincing' you must create for yourself and the other actors a convincing environment. This means that the way you use furniture, props, doors, even mere space, the way you look at imaginary objects – all these must be appropriate to the context.

You must learn when to move and when to keep still. Broadly speaking, you must not move when movement would seem unnatural or when a move on your part would draw attention away from something more relevant. For instance, if you are suddenly told a piece of horrifying news you do not, in real life, gesticulate. You may sit, even fall, but more probably for several seconds your whole energy will be concentrated on the message and its implications. Thereafter all sorts of movements and sounds may follow; but at first absolute stillness. There are times when it may be natural for the character whom you are playing to move, but when such movement would distract the focus of attention from something else on stage. You have to learn where, at any given moment, this focus should be, and why; and then learn appropriate ways, and appropriate moments, to shift it.

It is not always realized how easily an audience can be distracted. In ordinary life we accept a great deal of distraction both in sight and sound. Out of a complex of noise, out of many diverse, conspicuous objects, we select what is relevant and reject the rest. But this is not so in the theatre. The audience expects the selective process to have been achieved by the author and director; it expects to have the focus of its attention *directed* to what is relevant, and is easily distracted and irritated if irrelevant impressions are offered. Part of the audience's pleasure in the theatrical experience is that, at any given moment, something significant is happening. This may be no more than an intake of breath, the lifting of an eyebrow. It is intended to be significant. The audience knows this and resents the least distraction.

Of course there are moments when the focus is not so concentrated on a single effect: crowd-scenes, for instance, or group-scenes, like the murder of Julius Caesar, or the sort of ensemble which Chekhov presents, where some people are playing cards, others drinking tea, but where, at any moment, the focus must shift from the ensemble to one individual. Clearly at that moment it is highly inappropriate if one of those who is 'out of focus' pretends to play a trump or spills his tea. One keeps out of focus by avoiding any rapid or jerky movement or change of rhythm. Complete but unnatural stillness is almost more distracting than violent movement.

You must learn how to do only one important thing at a time. Beginners are for ever trying to run to the door, open it and react to what they see, with gesture, facial expression and audible sounds, all at the same time. You must plan a *sequence* of impressions for the audience. For instance, first indicate that something is happening outside the door. Second, go to the door and open it – the rhythm of these movements will be determined by the nature and urgency of the feeling. Third, look out. Be sure at this point to give the audience time to see you see whatever it is. Finally – react. This may take several seconds. But, if your ideas are intelligibly and feelingly expressed, they will be several interesting seconds for the audience and the tension, amusement or curiosity can be progressively played upon, that is to say the little sequence of impressions must be worked up to a peak. The beginner, frightened of a pause which he does not know how to fill, rushes through the business so fast that nothing is clear and the whole moment is a meaningless blur.

Therefore, to be 'convincing' in even a small part, you need to have not only some aptitude but to know quite a few tricks of the trade. And being 'convincing' is only the beginning of being a good actor. More important than merely to convince is to enlighten. The good actor reveals feelings and ideas and 'nuances' which are only implicit in the text. This means that he must be sufficiently imaginative to discover such implications and sufficiently skilful to express them.

Finally, a good actor must have a quality in his personality which commands the eyes and ears of an audience. The eye of an audience is not held solely by physical beauty – and, anyway, beauty lies in the eye of the beholder and can be considerably enhanced by artifice. Audiences look at actors who have some kind of magnetism. This is largely a matter of self-confidence on the actor's part, the belief that he is, in fact, worth looking at. Similarly, the ear of an audience inclines towards voices which are varied and expressive, rather than merely 'beautiful'. The Voice Beautiful is generally, alas, the Voice Dull. The people to whom one's ear is literally compelled to listen have not necessarily the sweetest, gentlest or even the loudest voices. Probably the most compelling appearances and voices are the most sexually potent; but here again nature can be powerfully reinforced by art.

Good acting, is, first, convincing; then, enlightening; finally, compelling. Likewise, bad acting is unconvincing, unenlightening and boring. I have known bad actors with compelling attributes: stunning physique, a magnificent voice. For this reason opera-singers and ballet-dancers can have highly successful careers and be simply terrible actors. I have known bad actors to succeed brilliantly in parts which permitted their very badness to be an advantage. I have known good actors, who through lack of taste or education, can only succeed when well-directed; and even more good actors who are prevented from being better by egotism, by being unable to realize that the whole of a work of art, in this case the performance of a play, must be greater than even the most brilliant of its parts.

Finally, let us remind ourselves that 'good' and 'bad' are exceedingly subjective terms. Nothing and no one is good all the time and in all circumstances. But a really good actor will never be utterly terrible in anything; and a really bad one, though he may do well in certain parts, will never cause an experienced observer to mistake success for talent.

★      ★      ★

*For beginners . . .*

Here are five practical 'tips'. They are not intended to be all-inclusive. The first is infinitely the most important. Learning to breathe is the basis of all acting. The meaningless pause (generally due to inadequate breath control) is the besetting and deadliest sin of bad acting. Fidgetting is the next most deadly. 4 and 5 are less basic; but I have noticed that most inexperienced actors need guidance on these points.

1 Before you say anything, or do anything, on the stage, TAKE A BREATH. The more deeply you have to feel, the more deeply must you breathe, quite apart from whether you have to speak or not.

   Don't take a breath when you hear your cue; you will then be late and create a meaningless pause (see 2 below). The breath should be taken when, probably from the previous speech of your partner, you get the idea which governs your own speech or reaction. A breath can, and usually should, be taken several seconds before you need it. It can easily be 'held' until required.

2 NEVER MAKE MEANINGLESS PAUSES. They usually occur when you take the breath which you have neglected to plan.

The deliberate, meaningful pause is usually more effective than any speech, and, if supported by breath and imagination, can nearly always be far longer than most beginners dare to make it. Again and again actors kill a meaningful pause by making a meaningless one just beforehand or just afterwards. Here is an example: 'I must tell you, Mr Fothergill, and it gives me nothing but shame and bitter grief to do so, that I am your long-lost child.' Mr Fothergill's reaction can be more theatrical if you pause before the *dénouement*, that is to say, if you pause before 'am your long-lost che-ild'. But nine inexperienced actors out of ten will kill this pause by making another one earlier. Thus: 'I must tell you, Mr Fothergill, (pause) and it gives me', etc. This meaningless pause (made because they haven't taken enough breath to get through the subsequent phrases) completely undermines the meaningful pause before 'am your long-lost che-ild'.

3 If there is no good reason to move, KEEP STILL. Inexperienced actors are apt to feel self-conscious if they are not doing something. Painfully conscious of large, red things on the ends of their arms, they Make Gestures.

WATCH people in real situations analogous to those in which you find yourself on stage. See how very little they actually do.

4 How you REACT to what your partners in a scene are saying or doing is frequently more important than what you yourself have to say or do.

5 Supposing, at a moment when the focus is meant to be elsewhere, that you have to make a movement (open a window or a door, put on a hat, stub out a cigarette). In order not to pull the focus on to yourself, move as slowly and smoothly as you can. It is rapid or jerky movements which pull the eye of the audience. At the same time you must not move in a falsely slow or obviously surreptitious manner; just do whatever you have to do as slowly and quietly as you *naturally* can.

The following are not 'tips' but facts, of which intending actors should be, but seldom are, aware:

1 A well-trained actor should be able to manage, at moderate speed and sufficiently loudly to 'carry' in a large theatre, SEVEN lines of blank verse.

Untrained, unpractised speakers are 'pumped' after one and a half lines.

2 A well-trained voice should easily cover a range of two and a half octaves. In normal conversation we rarely use more than one.

## Professional and amateur

The main difference between the professional and the amateur actor is that the former gets paid to act. Absolutely this does not mean that he is more talented or that he pays more attention to duty. However, I think that the professional tends to be more skilful because he gets more practice. If you play to the public several hundred times a year, you become almost sickeningly familiar with the behaviour of audiences; and, if you are bright, you consider not only how but why they react as they do and you adjust your performance accordingly. An experienced actor needs only to be on stage for a few seconds to take the measure of an audience. He will, almost automatically, make all manner of minute adjustments of pace, pitch, emphasis, all too subtle to upset the rehearsed rhythm and routine of the performance, but sufficient to make and maintain contact with each particular audience. For instance, a sophisticated audience can be trusted to pick up all sorts of implications and associations which will have to be emphasized and explained to a matinée audience of suburban housewives in over-bright hats. The emphasis and explanation will be managed by good actors with great tact. Indeed, a considerable part of an actor's skill and intuition is concerned with handling the audience tactfully, with gauging its collective capacity to grapple with the ideas which are being put forward, and then evoking a collective response a little more intelligent and sensitive than would be evoked by less tactful handling. 'Tactful', by the way, doesn't imply anything insincere or condescending. It's a question of being imaginatively *en rapport* with your audience, of not despising the matinée ladies because they are not so bright as their hats. The actor who feels dislike or contempt, rather than love, for his audience will never get far.

This matter of *rapport* is, of course, a two-way traffic. Just as the actors must establish a sympathetic relation with each audience, so the audience must accept what is offered and give back sympathy for sympathy. Every audience gets the performance which it deserves. A lively audience gets a lively performance, a dull audience a dull one. At the same time, dull audiences can be stimulated into liveliness and, I suppose, though I hope it happens less frequently, an audience may begin lively and be gradually stupefied by stupid goings-on.

It is the lack of *rapport* which makes it very hard, indeed scarcely possible, to achieve great acting on the screen or on television. We can, and quite often do, see immensely skilful and subtle performances. But, without the incandescence of an audience's instant and delighted come-back, the circuit of action and reaction, stimulus and response, is never complete. Without the aid of an audience, actors cannot achieve that little more, which is better than their conscious best. This is not just a matter of vain and nervous creatures craving the reassurance of laughter and applause. It is that the relation of actor to audience is essentially sociable. Imagine yourself making a thrilling recruiting speech in an empty room, or cracking an intimate, witty joke to a stone-deaf grandmother.

Compared with the professional, the amateur actor does not have as many opportunities to learn either to gauge an audience or to modify his performance accordingly. Nor does the amateur encounter so many different *kinds* of audience. Indeed one of his principal difficulties, especially in his early years, is that his audiences consist so largely of the same neighbours, friends, well-wishers and, worst of all, relations. Can anyone, however gifted, do himself justice in a scene, say, of passionate sexuality when the audience is dominated by the parents, grandparents, aunts and uncles of the Great Lover?

Again the professional has the amateur at a disadvantage, in that his acting has, or should have, first call upon his energy. It is hard for the amateur to do a day's work at some other job, and then, after a scrambled meal, to apply the necessary energy to the make-believe of a play. Of course it is a *change* of occupation and this may be extremely stimulating, especially if your bread-and-butter job is boring. But anyone who has worked with an amateur company knows how hard it is to achieve a full complement at every, even at any, rehearsal.

And the absentees are not so because of slackness but because their theatrical career is only a sideline. Hamlet, who is a doctor, has been called to deliver not a soliloquy but a baby; Laertes has been sent by his firm to Antwerp; Rosencrantz is required for overtime in the shipyard; Ophelia is a bridesmaid at her twin sister's wedding and the Queen has a child in bed with mumps. That just about washes out the first run-through of *Hamlet* and throws a carefully planned schedule to the wolves.

Another strike against the amateur theatre: even the largest most sophisticated amateur groups have almost insuperable casting difficulties connected with every production. And, even when there is a choice, producers are dogged by problems of 'fair do's': Poppy had the lead in the last show, therefore, though Poppy is obviously the first choice for this one, we must give the part to Jasmine. Jasmine is a little too old and a great deal too fat, but her husband is outstandingly the best actor in the district and we simply can't afford to risk a joint resignation.

I will not say that in a professional production problems of casting do not exist. Quite obviously they do. For example, at any given time the actors in the entire English-speaking theatre, who combine the ability to play a great heroic part – Othello, say, or Brand or Tamburlaine – with the celebrity to justify critical and public confidence in their choice, can be counted on the fingers of a single mutilated hand. Sir John Olivier, Sir Ralph Clements, Mr Marlon Plummer are all engaged; Sir Laurence Gielgud doesn't like the part; Sir Bernard Guinness doesn't like the leading lady who once referred to him publicly as Humpty-Dumpty. Eventually we have no choice but to offer the part to an actor who began as Number Eighteen on our list. But at least there were eighteen possibilities. In the amateur theatre the producer is amazingly fortunate if there are three.

## Male and female

The difference between male and female has, I guess, never been quite so great as has at certain epochs been supposed. And the theatre has always had an attraction for rather lady-like gentlemen and rather manly ladies.

I presume one of the reasons for this is that in the theatre sexually inverted people can to a great extent create an environment of fantasy to suit themselves and avoid the cruel hostility with which 'normal' men and women too often regard sexual inversion. In the tolerant, unstable, itinerant world of the theatre it is easier to be 'queer' than in more stable and conventional institutions, like General Motors or the Church of England. For my part, I think that its tolerance and ability to make use of the weirdest characters and talents is one of the most attractive features of the stage. But to be fair both to the Automotive Industry and to Organized Religion, they do, even in my limited experience, find room in their ranks for a creditable number of creatures who could by no stretch of the imagination be considered 'normal'.

Transvestite goings-on have always been one of the long suits – no, I think I mean strong points – of the stage. In the Elizabethan, as in the classical Greek theatre, the actors were all of the male sex, and the women's parts were played by men. A frequent comedic device in Shakespeare is to have a Girl played by a Boy, who then dresses up and pretends to be a boy and then finally reverts to his/her original feminine assumption. *The Merchant of Venice, Twelfth Night, As You Like It* all rely heavily on this device. Portia, Viola or Rosalind are now played not by boys, but by leading ladies of the mature experience which we expect nowadays from the exponents of long, difficult rôles in artificial comedy. Yet let us admit that for leading ladylike accomplishments and charisma we pay a rather high price in plausibility and fun.

In Shakespeare's day there were boy-players, apprenticed to theatrical companies from a very early age, highly-trained and, by twelve or thirteen years old, quite experienced and skilful professionals, who could evidently cope more than adequately with the technical demands of Rosalind, perhaps even with those of Cleopatra or Lady Macbeth.

Nowadays we have, and I think very rightly, far stricter regulations about the employment of youngsters of school age. It simply is not conceivable that in Great Britain a boy could now have theatrical experience comparable to that of the boys in Shakespeare's and Burbage's time. In the United States, where the regulations are as yet much less strict, it is just imaginable that a child should be available for such training, but, at present, utterly inconceivable that the training should be directed towards serious or classical work, rather than towards vaudeville, musicals, television or films.

A few years ago the National Theatre of Great Britain staged *As You Like It* with young men in the female parts. It was a charming production and I have never heard anyone fault it for poor taste or indelicacy. But the parts were played not by children but by grown-up actors, pretending to be young boys, playing girls. They did it skilfully, subtly. They were amply good enough to demonstrate how much more amusing these boy–girl parts could be, if played by the marvellously trained, but still childish, original exponents. But the very skill of the National Theatre actors, and the taste with which they avoided the least suggestion of the vulgarly epicene, fought against the simplicity and freshness and fun which only real children could have brought to the parts.

Nowadays, with rare exceptions like this *As You Like It*, transvestism only survives professionally in night-club acts, in vaudeville and in pantomime. Male impersonators, of whom probably the most famous was Vesta Tilley, with her gallery of trim little soldiers and exquisitely languid 'Swells', were, in its palmy days around the turn of this century, pillars of vaudeville. Today women impersonating men have rather been eclipsed by men impersonating women, currently a very usual night-club attraction. Those whom I have seen do not attempt to be comic so much as lusciously beautiful; and I do not think that they aim to fascinate sexually inverted men, but rather to fascinate all-comers in an almost sexless impersonal way. The point of the impersonation is its detached and intricate skill. The spectator is asked to note the comment upon provocative strip-tease, rather than to be provoked.

The surviving stronghold of transvestism is the English Christmas Pantomime. In this strange and liturgical form of Pop-Art the Hero is invariably played by a female – a big strapping lass in tights and jerkin. The costume varies little, whether its wearer pretends to be Prince Dandini (black silk tights; black velvet jerkin, heavily spangled; tricorn hat; lace ruffles and high-heeled patent pumps; all intended, I think, to suggest an eighteenth-century Beau) or Dick Whittington (rustic straw hat; jerkin vaguely reminiscent of a rustic smock; bundle and stick to suggest travel) or Aladdin (pyramidal hat; jacket in 'oriental' printed cotton; flat canvas 'coolie' shoes.)

The Principal Boy woos the Principal Girl, a soprano of softy cuddly type in frilly pink, who has almost no 'lines' but is entrusted with the best of the sentimental songs. Then there is the Principal Boy's Confidant, another big strapping Miss dressed like a boy, only less expensively. The Confidant doesn't have much to do except to lend an ear as the Boy unfolds a rather sketchy and ramshackle plot. Occasionally, however, the Confidant has a line which is meant to cue-in a production number: 'Oo, girls, isn't it gorgeous to be guests at the Royal Ball!' to which the chorus (girls about twelve-years-old trained by a local dancing mistress) squeak in unison: 'Ow, yus, jus' gor-juss', whereat the orchestra strikes up and they express their joy in a clog dance in two-four, *molto allegro*. But ultimately the Panto stands or falls by the performance of the Dame (Cinderella's wicked stepmother or Aladdin's Mum). The Dame is played by a man – a low comedian of ripe experience. It's a poor evening if the Dame's drawers don't come down or if 'She' doesn't get caught up in a knockabout act involving china-smashing or papering the parlour.

American audiences would be amazed, I fancy, at what they would call the 'earthiness' of the Dame's jokes – utterly frank references to bed-pans, diapers or toilet paper; and homely songs comparing the Dame's old husband to a kettle without a spout. These are received with yells of delight by 'family' audiences and huge parties of workmates out on an annual spree.

Alas, pantomime, is on the way 'out'. Once, every theatre in England, except the very posh metropolitan houses, put on its own 'panto' at Christmas. Now, year by year, the number dwindles. As the old vaudeville comics gradually grow old and die, the quality of the entertainment is changing. Rumbustious proletarian jollity is giving way to the electronic slickness and suburban gentility of night-club comedians and television personalities.

But even yet pantomime is based on the topsyturvy saturnalian joke of dressing men as women, women as men. It is a simple joke which has survived from the earliest days of classical Greek theatre, and will survive long after pantomime, as we have known it, has gone the way of the Comedia dell'Arte.

The old joke is still the mainstay of difficult jollifications – Gala Night on the Luxury Cruise; Family Christmas in Resort Hotels. Paper hats are put on, exchanged and re-exchanged. Papa appears now as a witch, a cowboy, a baby and Mae West; plump Mama convulses her brood when she makes to hornpipe in a sailor's cap.

Mention of the National Theatre's all-male *As You Like It* reminds me of an all-female *Twelfth Night* of some years ago.

It is an ironic fact that, while Shakespeare wrote for a cast of men, it is casts of women who are now, at all events in the amateur field, more eager to present his plays. This *Twelfth Night* was got up by a Women's Rural Institute in a remote part of East Anglia. The Village Hall was what is called an All-Purpose Auditorium, that is to say that it was truly suitable for no specific purpose. In the manner of such halls the stage was raised about four feet above the level of the unraked floor. Thus in the front rows the spectators could not see performers below the knee (in this case, just as well); after the first row or two the spectators' view was restricted to brief glimpses between the heads of those in front.

The lighting, ingeniously contrived with biscuit tins, left the stage in a sullen twilight and concentrated brilliantly on a gap between two wings, painted to suggest a woodland glade. Through the gap could be descried a door marked Ladies. Every time it opened a spring-hinge gave a long, agonized squeal and every time it closed the hinge squealed again. As the cast was large and understandably nervous, the door opened and shut about seven times a minute.

As always with a great dramatic masterpiece, excellencies easily outshone the inadequacies of amateur performance. Choreography there was none: the characters just stood in a line and faced not one another but the audience. Yet talent could be easily distinguished from non-talent, and, because the general level was low, the two or three talented performances seemed more brilliant than one ever sees in a professional production. A bishop's widow was tremendous as Sir Toby; and Orsino, because the young girl who played him was truly gifted, was easily able to surmount a rather strange first impression. Each lady had been responsible for her own costume and Orsino was in lilac satin knickers worn under a black tail coat in which her father was wont to collect the offertory in church. For me she clinched the point that there is something very 'right' about transvestite acting. There was something so clever and fantastic and, in a true sense, serious about this young girl pretending in her ridiculous get-up to be a man. It was fantasy and poetry where theatrical realism is just dull old prose. It achieved plausibility against great odds. And, for my money, that is far more interesting than just being plain plausible.

Naturally, I am not suggesting that young dukes should always be played by girls in their fathers' coats. Merely that when they bring it off they achieve a *tour de force*; and *tours de force* are a not unimportant drop of the theatre's life-blood.

*Straight and character*

To play 'straight' is to appear without disguise, speaking in your own voice, wearing the sort of clothes you might wear yourself, doing all you can to turn the part into yourself rather than to turn yourself into the part. 'Character' acting, on the other hand, presupposes exactly the reverse, that you put on a disguise, assume a voice and so on, in order to create a character which has small resemblance to yourself.

In a sense, all acting is character acting, since, even in parts expressly written for them, actors are not quite playing themselves, and even the straightest actors only want to reveal certain aspects of themselves. What the straight actor presents is a sort of glorified image of what he hopes he looks and sounds like, an idealized portrait with the more attractive features stressed, the less attractive minimized.

On the whole, straight actors make more money and become more celebrated than character actors. After all, the public, even the theatre-going public, is much less interested in acting than in personalities. Very few people after they have seen a performance are capable of criticism above the level of, 'I liked him' and 'She was sweet, especially in her pink'. Of course, it gets a bit monotonous always appearing as your radiant self, always beautiful, always charming. And as the years roll on, the strain becomes inexorably greater, until gradually you turn from being the glass of fashion and the mould of form into a sort of monstrosity about whom still hang the airs and graces of youth, but not convincingly: the charm, like the complexion, is synthetic.

I knew an actress who continued, for financial reasons, to play nubile heroines well into her seventies. Towards the end of her very distinguished career, audiences, not unnaturally, began to fall away. But not at matinées. These would be crowded by other very old ladies, fighting for the seats nearest to the stage. Peering through opera-glasses, they would try to see 'how it was done', gloating when they discovered tiny stitch-marks, which indicated plastic surgery, gleefully noting the adhesive tape which held this or that in place. After the performance not one of them could have told you a witty line or a good situation in the play. But every single one could, and did, regale herself and friends with tea and cakes and grisly details of the stratagems and martyrdoms by means of which the poor old actress was endeavouring to hold at bay the enemy – their enemy as well as hers. But, instead of regarding her as their ally in the battle, she was a laughing-stock, because they were 'really' young – oh yes, still really young and attractive, whereas she was only a silly actress pretending.

And this, at last, is the fate of all the stars who put more confidence in charm and beauty than in skill or industry. It is the fate also of those who may have skill and industry, but who have found it convenient, or indeed often necessary, to understress these in favour of easy popularity. Eventually they find that their 'fans' are fickle and their worship not exactly insincere but ambivalent. Side by side with the love which 'fans' offer to 'stars' exists envy. There', thinks the fan, 'go I, if I had his (or her) opportunity.' For they think it's just a matter of luck, and so, though not quite as much as they think, to a great extent it is.

So, on the whole, it is the 'character' people who have the best life in the theatre. And I have noticed that most of those who are drawn seriously to the stage (I do not mean musical comedy or films or television) are not anxious to display themselves for admiration, but to hide themselves and what they believe to be their inadequacy behind the disguise of character parts and to take refuge from the real world in a world of make-believe. And while for the character man the rewards in celebrity and money are much smaller, there is the prospect of a more interesting life. First, because there is far more variety in his parts. Second, because if he is skilful and reliable he becomes, as the years pass, more employable, not less, since he is not so dependent on good looks and sex appeal. Third, because he is not so subject as the star to the pressures of publicity and fame; sex-maddened fans do not tear off his fly-buttons for souvenirs. Finally, because his work, though not spectacularly lucrative, enables him to live as comfortably as a reasonably successful lawyer or businessman, but permits him a far more varied routine both in time and place.


## Legit and mass-media

There used to be a kind of acting called 'legitimate' to distinguish it from the 'lyric' or musical theatre and from vaudeville. Nowadays, the 'legit' means acting in a 'straight' (that is, non-musical play) to living human beings rather than to a camera or microphone. The obvious technical difference between acting to people in a theatre and acting before a camera is that in the theatre what you do must be visible, and what you say audible, to people perhaps as much as thirty or forty yards away; whereas for close-ups – and almost every important moment of acting in films or television is shot in close-up – the camera and microphone are no more than inches away from the actor. This greatly simplifies the merely technical problems of acting to camera and microphone. The great thing is to seem 'natural'. It is also desirable to be imaginative, but this is hardly a technical matter.

In the theatre it is hard to be 'broad' enough. Life-size is not large enough and the beginner has constantly to be exhorted to speak more loudly, to mime more boldly. This presupposes not merely a good loud voice, but some skill in enunciation and pronunciation as well as some knowledge of how to direct the breath-stream. The beginner in films or television, on the other hand, especially if accustomed to the stage, is apt to act far too broadly, to speak too emphatically, to move his face too much, to smile or scowl in a life-sized manner, forgetting that, in movies anyway, his image will eventually be gigantically enlarged, so that on the screen his would-be engaging grin will become a volcanic eruption: two monstrous cheeks reft apart to reveal a double row of off-white manilla envelopes.

I suspect that it is easier to learn to do less than to learn to do more. Another point, in films and television each 'take' is of short duration. To shoot a scene for as long as five minutes is quite rare and quite an achievement; whereas in the theatre you have to keep going for the duration of the act, rarely less than twenty-five and often as long as fifty minutes.

This again means that the demands of the theatre are greater both upon technique and concentration. Concentration in the film or television studio is easier to achieve. For the brief period of the 'take' all other activity ceases. A bell clangs, red lights glow, and the studio, which a moment ago was a buzz of activity, with dozens, maybe a hundred people busy with lights, scenery, costumes, make-up, hairdressing or administrative duties, suddenly falls silent and utterly still. For the period of the 'take' everyone is intensely concentrated upon the performers. This is their moment, the peak up to which all the previous activity has been leading.

In a theatrical performance there is a good deal to distract the actors. Near at hand, although in comparative darkness, are other actors waiting to enter: property men preparing the banquet for Act Two; the stage-manager having a sibilant altercation with a late-arriving understudy. You must concentrate and firmly repress the passionate and very natural desire to know whether the understudy is pleading the missed bus, the broken alarm-clock or the aunt's funeral. And out front there are distractions too. At least twelve people are exhibiting the very noisiest symptoms of bad colds; programmes are rustling, so are sweet wrappings; latecomers have ruined the beginning of the play, earlygoers will ruin its end. There is a well-known story of a young actress making her first-ever professional appearance at a matinée in Eastbourne. Before the poor thing could speak her first 'line', she heard the audience set up a long, low continuous hiss. The young beginner died a thousand deaths, only to learn when she came off that the noise had been caused by five hundred old ladies whispering to one another: 'She's Gladys Cooper's sister, Doris.'

Again, in films, if something goes wrong, if a wine-glass breaks or someone's toupée comes unstuck, you simply 'cut', replace the broken glass, the lost dignity and begin again. But the very ease with which difficulties can be surmounted, not by ingenuity or intelligence, or some little Dutch Boy Shoving his Hand into the Dyke, but simply by spending apparently inexhaustible money and limitless time – the very ease of it all is deceptive. It turns out that in art – and, I suspect in every human undertaking – too much ease and liberty produces even deadlier results than too little. Limitations challenge the energetic person; the liberty derived from huge budgets and over-lenient supervision is an enervating drug.

This may seem to be the 'sour grapes' attitude of a disappointed elderly Puritan. Perhaps it is. But I seem to remember so many gifted and promising people whose promise has been blasted and whose gifts corrupted from the very moment that they 'got into the money'. With artists, as soon as they can buy their way out of artistic difficulties, pay 'experts' to solve problems which once they had to solve themselves by ingenuity, use electronic gadgets instead of their own imagination – from that moment, however commercially successful they may be, they are finished as artists.

And this brings us to the final difference between the theatre and the mass-media – the economic difference. Once the theatre was the sole means of distributing drama. (I discount the study of drama in universities and schools, which has always been almost wholly a literary not a theatrical activity.) Now the theatre has been completely outstripped economically, and in many important ways technically too, by mass-distributive and mechanical means of production. That the theatre will survive does not seem relevant here, where we are discussing acting, rather than drama in general, and, especially, the differences between acting to an audience present in a theatre as opposed to acting to camera and microphone for an audience which may, or even may not ever exist, according to circumstances almost entirely out of the actor's control.

If an actor aims primarily to act to camera and microphone, he will reach more people. He will, therefore, be liable to make more money and achieve a higher degree of celebrity, even if the term of that celebrity be alarmingly short. And these results can be had with a lower degree of technical accomplishment than if he were to direct his efforts primarily towards the theatre. It is also arguable that, because of the enormously wider distribution of his product, he can exercise more influence on the minds and hearts of the human race. In point of mere numbers, this is, of course, indisputable; but while statistics may give a reasonably reliable notion of the quantity of people who react to a given stimulus, they are far from reliable about the *degree* or *quality* of that reaction.

The theatre offers lower rewards to the actor in money and short-term celebrity. But in so far as it aims at a smaller but more serious audience, an audience which is prepared to concentrate more energy on the performance, in short, an élite as opposed to a mass-audience, the theatre must offer a more serious and energy-demanding programme; consequently it is a more challenging field for the actor. I hope that it is clear that the term 'élite' does not imply an audience exclusively composed of highly-born or highly-educated or even rich people. It simply implies an audience which is prepared to discriminate in its choice of entertainment, which isn't bamboozled by the ballyhoo of commerce, and which is prepared to realize that theatre is a co-operative effort between performers and audience from whom, therefore, considerable concentration and energy are demanded.

As it steadily continues to lose ground in the economic battle with the mass-distributive media, the theatre will depend more and more upon the classics of drama, less and less upon new work, which, economically as well as artistically, is far more of a risk. New work tends to be the work of young writers; and unless public subsidy for the theatre increases at a very much greater rate than I anticipate, young authors will not be able to disregard the vastly greater financial rewards and the vastly greater opportunities to establish a reputation which the mass-distributive media offer.

At the same time these media depend upon a mass-audience which, by definition, demands what is easily accessible to all kinds and conditions of people. Work of this character is hardly likely to be enduring. The young author already begins to be confronted by a choice. Shall he aim at the 'popular' audience, which wants something easy, unoriginal, uncontroversial (none of which necessarily means contemptible) or shall he aim at the élite audience which, for all its virtues, is all too ready to mistake snobbery for merit? Ideally he should aim at neither. He should write what interests himself. But if you are a young author with a wife and children to support you can't be too choosy. Some young writers aim at the popular market and hope to sell there something of which they need not be ashamed, the success of which might put them in a position to write what they want. The danger here is that they repeat in later works the 'popular' quality of earlier; and, having once rejected serious or difficult ideas, can never again achieve them.

What has all this to do with the actor? Plenty. Where the authors lead, the actors perforce follow. They must learn to act in the 'style' which is set by the authors. Just as the authors are being faced by a clearer-cut choice than, so it seems, some other generations have had to face, so are the actors: shall I offer myself in the market of popular entertainment, with inevitable compromises with triviality and commonness? Or shall I aim at the very much more economically limited and technically demanding field of the 'legit'?

Of course it still is and will, I think, continue to be possible to have a foot in both camps. Successful stage actors are still the aristocrats of the profession, for the good reason that they tend to be technically better equipped and imaginatively more sophisticated. And against the short-term fame of the popular star must be set the fact that long-term fame can only be achieved in the classical parts. You cannot compare Mr X in a performance of some ephemeral play of fifty years ago with Mr Y in a similar play today or with Mr Z in a similar play fifty years hence. But there *is* some possibility of comparing – and some point in so doing – Olivier's Hamlet with that of Gielgud, or of Maurice Evans, or of Alec Guinness or of Christopher Plummer; or that of Barrymore, Irving, Booth, Macready, Kean or Garrick.

I think one of the most moving performances of my theatre-going experience was that of Laurette Taylor in *The Glass Menagerie*. But where the technical demands on the actress were small, where greatness, nobility, vehement passion were not in place, to say that on this showing she was a great actress would be unjustified. Laurette Taylor's very successful career was achieved by being utterly charming in pieces like *Peg o' my Heart*, written to exploit her particular qualities, with no pretentions beyond being 'a hit'. To be a great actor or actress you must have been seen in a number of great parts. To be exquisitely poignant in a single poetic but essentially slight piece, like *The Glass Menagerie*, just is not enough.

Seriously ambitious actors want to feel that there may be a possibility of being remembered as great. They are not content just to be popular, rich and to conquer in parts which do not invite comparison with the giants of the past. Nor will such actors be attracted because film and television acting, compared to stage acting, makes small technical demands. Greatly talented people are high-spirited; they will always, as they always have, accept the challenge of difficulties and spurn the easy way and the soft environment.

# 3 *Teaching and learning*

*Can acting be taught?*

No art can be 'learned' by a person who has no talent in that particular field.

You can teach an untalented, unmusical child the elements of the pianoforte, but only the technical elements. Stern discipline and rigorous practice can, with great agony both for teacher and pupil, produce accurate and agile playing, but if the student has no basic musical gift the result is only a meagre reward for the pains.

It is the same with acting. Unless the student has both inclination and aptitude, all that a teacher can achieve is a quite sterile technical basis.

But a wise teacher can be exceedingly helpful to an eager and talented theatrical beginner. He can be taught to discipline his imagination; to develop both mind and body by practice; he can be taught quite a good deal about theatrical technique; he can be helped to develop his technique by developing the imagination and, no less important, vice versa. No teacher can create imagination in the soul of a student. But then it is doubtful whether anyone is wholly devoid of imagination, and a teacher can stimulate one which is otherwise sluggish. It is, however, questionable whether the tremendous effort, on both sides, is justified. In my opinion, the aim of an acting school, as of all education, should be to help the student to teach himself.

*Relation of acting teacher and student*

The relation between master and pupil, as with all teaching, is highly subjective. Dr X may be an admirable teacher, in general, and will hold the interest of nearly all his students and inspire them with a desire to do well. But, even so, there will be a few with whom Dr X, kind, understanding and lucid as he may be, can make no contact. His personality and theirs can establish no satisfactory relationship. In subjects which involve a good deal of technical as well as theoretical instruction, such as surgery, dentistry, music or drama, the *rapport* between master and pupil becomes of dominant importance.

Take singing, for instance: the relationship between singing-teacher and pupil is dominated, especially in the early stages, by technique, by such matters as breath-control and voice placement. Now no two students have exactly the same vocal mechanism and, up to now at any rate, the terminology in which pupil and master communicate is vague and figurative. 'Lean the voice against the back of the eyes,' one celebrated singing teacher used to say, and to some of his students this injunction was perfectly intelligible, though obviously not in a literal way. The metaphor made sense and helped them to direct the breath-stream as the teacher desired. To others it was only confusing and got them nowhere.

There is no universally applicable rule of thumb which will infallibly direct the breath-stream correctly, or indeed direct far simpler acts. There is no universally correct way of peeling an apple. There are just some ways which are generally considered less incorrect than others. Since the anatomy of the vocal mechanism differs, often radically, from singer to singer, it must follow that the vocal method which has greatly helped A to improve his voice-placement may be no help at all to B and may even have a ruinous effect on poor C. Yet most singing-teachers are convinced, on the evidence of their own success as singers, reinforced by successes with the majority of their pupils, that they have A Method. It is hard to convince them, even on the evidence of poor C's destroyed career, that their method is not 'correct' and therefore not universally applicable. They will never admit disaster in the case of C. They will most honourably admit their share in it; it is scarcely ever maintained that the wreck of his voice was solely C's fault. But they believe the failure to have been one of communication: 'C and I just couldn't get along – couldn't understand each other.' They refuse, however, to admit that the method itself should never have been tried on poor C.

The teaching and learning of acting is not considered so subjective a business as the teaching of singing and instrumental playing, because the technical demands are not considered so exacting. It is harder to learn to sing, it is maintained, than to learn to speak. Everyone, it is maintained, can speak, but a singing voice is a rare gift and must be trained.


## Speaking and singing

I am not satisfied that this is so. A voice is a voice is a voice. Singing is merely speech raised to a higher power – a more sustained line and a wider range, both of pitch and volume, than is customary in ordinary conversation. The same instrument is used for all vocal activities. But it is used in various ways. Singing apart, we use our 'speaking' voice quite variously. You speak in a certain manner to someone who has just had a severe illness; you wouldn't get far if you spoke in that 'voice' to a mass-meeting of angry strikers.

The voice, as the singer uses it, demands more technique than the voice as used in ordinary conversation. Acting comes somewhere in between. The technical demands are greater than for ordinary conversation, less than for singing. On the other hand the imaginative demands on the actor tend to be greater than those on the singer.

Take the text of a spoken 'aria' – a soliloquy from *Hamlet*, for example, or the epilogue to *The Tempest*, or Saint Joan's recantation, after she has been sentenced to perpetual imprisonment. There are no precise instructions to the speaker. There are, in fact, no instructions at all. The interpretation has to be inferred from the context, from the nature of the character and the situation in which he finds himself, furthermore the technical guides are minimal. Melody, pace, pitch, volume and colour are at the sole discretion of the actor. Rhythm, both in the blank verse and in Shaw's prose, is, to a very limited extent, suggested.

Now take an operatic aria. Melody is indicated with absolute precision; rhythm hardly less precisely; volume, pace and phrasing, including such details as the stress upon any given syllable, are not precisely ordered, but there is very little latitude permitted. Only in the matter of vocal colouring is the singer completely free to express himself. The actor is called upon for far more intellectual effort. He supplies a great deal more invention. But, fairly enough, the vocal technique required of the actor is less than that which a singer must supply. Nor, with a very few notable exceptions, do the speeches, even in rhetorical plays, call for such vocal feats as are needed not just in Wagner or Verdi but even in comparatively undemanding *Lieder*.

This means that we require a much higher standard of vocal competence from quite minor singers than we demand from even the greatest actors. Today the two greatest actors on the English-speaking stage are widely considered to be John Gielgud and Laurence Olivier. Of the two, Gielgud, although the range of his acting is smaller than Olivier's, is the more sophisticated rhetorician. When he is suited by the material, he speaks with a matchless musicality. No one, whom I have ever heard, comes near him for aptness and variety of melody, elegance of phrasing, subtlety of rhythm. Yet the voice has never been developed to its full potential. Well-produced in the middle, the top and bottom are a little weak and strangulated. This in a singer would prevent his getting anywhere near the top of his profession. Olivier, also extremely musical (I don't think it's possible to be an important actor without a strong musical talent), has developed, as he expresses it himself, the brass of his orchestra but never mastered the strings. That is to say, he commands marvellous tones for violent, exciting vocal crises and challenges, but the soft, tender, luscious tones are considerably less marvellous; or, to put it technically, nasal resonance has been cultivated at the expense of the deeper softer resonances of chest and throat.

There are reasons why the actor does not work at vocal technique as seriously as the singer. For one thing, it is a laborious life's work; for another, the untrained voice is almost as serviceable as the trained. In most parts in most plays, he can 'get by' without much training. Finally, it is widely and erroneously believed that careful cultivation of the voice leads to the production of the 'pear-shaped tones' which American actors put on when they want to mock the British, to listening to one's own voice, to concentrating on method not meaning, and to the ultimate, the barely-to-be-mentioned, the unnatural and unforgivable histrionic sin of Elocution.

There is nothing whatever wrong with elocution. In fact, it is essential to elocute if you want to communicate clearly and expressively. The sin is bad elocution. Similarly it is not the cultivation of vocal technique which produces pear-shaped tones and ham acting. It is miscultivation.

*How essential is vocal training?*

I admit that actors can get by with murderously uncultivated voices, so long as they stick to naturalistic plays or films in which 'Ugh!' and 'Huh!' do duty for more sophisticated utterances. But let it always be remembered that the greatest plays do demand, maybe only now and then but now and then at the moments of greatest importance, that the actor really let fly, really give 'the works' to rhetorical set-pieces. Remember that dramatic masterpieces just are *not* naturalistic, are *not* life-sized, are *not* about you and me and the Joneses. They are about Great People faced with Great Issues.

Just as singing is speech raised to a higher power, so is great drama the raising of real life to a higher power. Indeed drama is great just in so far as it is larger, louder, more high-powered and high-coloured than the drab little existence which is all that we know of real life, until a great artist gives us a notion of how it might conceivably look and feel and sound. Therefore, if an actor is going to be content to spend his professional life interpreting life-sized people in little and predominantly trumpery little plays, there really is no good reason why he should bother with the interminable and exhausting task of making the best of his vocal equipment. But for the seriously ambitious actor there is every reason. In the theatre, as opposed to films and television or even literature, communication occurs predominantly by means of the spoken word.

His voice is by far the most important weapon in the actor's armoury. A dull or a plain face can be transformed by paint and putty and, even more effectively, by a lively expression; a good tailor can do wonders for a poor figure; the sexiest men and women are often the dullest actors; allure can be simulated, and often is, by persons of the most meagre physique and frigid temperament. But nothing, nothing, nothing can disguise a dull voice dully produced; just as nothing can thrill an audience like a noble voice nobly produced.

'I might believe all this,' I think I hear you say, 'about the crucial importance of vocal training, but I have heard a great singer attempt to make a speech. The noise, quite apart from the matter, was puny and unimportant.'

It is a point. But I don't think it invalidates my argument.

I myself, when very young, was privileged to hear Melba 'speak' on a public occasion. Apart from the fact that she talked absolute bosh, she barked like an elderly sea-captain and in a raucous Australian accent. But God in His almighty wisdom and fairness rarely sees fit to lavish all his gifts upon one person. So comes it that athletes, who look like Greek Gods, too often have the intellectual capacities of nine-year-old children; that world-renowned professors tend to flat chests and thick glasses. Thus the handsomest, the wisest or the liveliest of His creatures are rarely gifted also with great voices. Also, when a great singer makes a speech, it does not follow that the speech will be wise or interesting or amusing, or even well-delivered. Great singers are trained to interpret music which, as we have discussed, permits very narrow latitude for their invention. They are quite unaccustomed to make up not only their own words, but their own melody, rhythm, pace, pitch and phrasing. Small wonder if their efforts are sometimes a little amateurish.

*The training of actors in the United States*

In Great Britain the training of actors is almost entirely confined to Trade Schools, if I may describe them so without any intention of derogating their status. They are mostly centred in, or near, London, and still aim a bit more than I think wise to enable their students to fulfil the kind of demands which are likely to be made by theatrical managers and the television and film companies. Very likely this is the most honest way in which they can discharge their duty to the students, most of whom want above all to be effectually merchandised. But I find the training directed a little too much towards what is believed to be useful *now*, rather than trying to sort out what is temporarily from what is perenially useful in a theatrical training.

In Britain drama is only just beginning to be considered a suitable subject to be taught at university level. There are at present very few university departments, and these few do not regard themselves as Trade Schools for the profession. Rather they are endeavouring to make their students take an intelligent, but largely theoretic, interest in drama as an adjunct to the cultivation of a well-educated person.

In the United States, on the other hand, universities are by far the most important centres of theatrical training. Compared with those of Great Britain the American universities tend to offer a far more pragmatic education, less concerned with learning for its own sake than with handing its students practical equipment for the battle of life, which is still, in spite of a prevailing but still new affluence, regarded very much as an economic battle.

At present some thousands of colleges reckon drama as one of the major subjects for which 'credits' are allotted: the B.A. degree depends upon getting a required number of credits. The drama courses, in comparison with Middle English or Higher Mathematics, Applied Psychology or even Economics, are widely regarded as 'fun courses'. Every year, therefore, a staggering number of young people graduate with drama as one of their major subjects. Tens of thousands of these have never seen a professional dramatic production, for the excellent reason that they have never in their lives been within five hundred miles of a professional theatre. Hundreds of thousands have never seen a professional production of a classical play, because, even if they are within range of a professional theatre, American theatres hardly ever present classical works.

A very few colleges are now beginning to stiffen their casts with professional actors-in-residence. But this is quite expensive and puts such a project way out of the reach of the vast majority of schools. Indeed so lowly are drama departments rated by the Boards of Regents of many, if not most, colleges, that the university theatre gets no allocation of funds, but is expected to pay its way. The result of this is that drama professors, if they wish their department to survive, are forced to save the financial day by putting on, as part of the drama curriculum, Broadway musicals of yesteryear. These are supposed to, and frequently do, recoup the losses incurred by the 'educational' production of plays by bores like Shakespeare, Molière, Ibsen, Shaw, O'Neill or, that most lethal poison of the American college box-office, Harold Pinter.

So long as their theatre must pay its way, it is hard to see what else the professors can do. *Paint your Wagon* or *Pal Joey*, with students in the star rôles, a student chorus, a faculty wife 'at' the piano (or, in a really bang-up effort two faculty wives 'at' two pianos), a director who is the toast of the *Tulane Review* but who hasn't seen a Broadway production since Ethel Merman was a girl, scenery and costumes faculty-designed, student-executed on half a shoestring . . . if they were getting it up for fun in their spare time, well, God bless 'em. But to offer this as the crowning glory of an educational programme, which will count heavily towards the B.A. degree . . . well, that doesn't seem to be at all the ticket.

Now, every year, around twenty thousand young Americans graduate after taking drama as their major course. Of these, professional theatre may perhaps absorb two hundred in a year, though I should think that is a very generous estimate. A high proportion of the remainder become drama teachers, either at college, junior college, high school or primary level.

Thus the ranks of drama teachers swell at an annual rate which is alarming to contemplate. Now, while it is true that demand creates supply, it is also true that, to some limited extent, supply creates demand. Every year the vested interest of drama education becomes larger, as every year more and more recruits flock to the colours. So every year more and ever more jobs are found for drama instructors, recreation directors, leisure supervisors, and so on. I do not say that this is a bad thing: it is vital that wise uses of leisure time be explored. But I cannot help feeling that they should, in the dramatic field, be explored by people better qualified than drama majors, whose training and experience has rarely transcended a quite unambitious and wholly amateurish college level. It is not, of course, that any special virtue is attached to the label 'professional'. But the stiff competition, which exists in the professional theatre, tends to winnow the chaff from the wheat. In the academic theatre there is a tendency for staff appointments to go not to the most talented applicants but to those with the best academic qualifications. Talent and scholarship do not always go together.

It should be mentioned that in the United States there exist a certain number of dramatic Trade Schools. Their quality, like that of a school of any kind in any part of the world, varies greatly from time to time and is greatly dependent upon the calibre of the head person. The fact that they are completely outnumbered by university departments and also that the professional theatre is so very much centred on New York, makes their influence proportionately rather smaller than that of their British counterparts.

Perhaps I should also mention that I have never met a British drama student who did not yearn for an American school. This would be more comprehensible if I had ever met an American drama student who did not yearn with equal ardour for a British school.

One more point before we leave the drama departments of American colleges: it is an ironic fact that, in every part of the country, even in quite remote, unlikely little institutions, there exist elaborately and expensively equipped university theatres. On the whole, the college amateurs operate in far better material surroundings than their professional brethren. This is because in New York the value of land is so enormous that theatres occupy only cramped sites; and because the demand for theatres is still much greater than the supply, which dwindles year by year, the owners can afford to rent them in run-down condition on terms which force the tenant to supply all portable equipment. Outside New York, the commercial touring theatre, like the American railroads, is fighting with antiquated, run-down equipment, a desperate and demoralized rearguard action against total elimination. The colleges, on the other hand, receive gifts and bequests from rich alumnae, which enable them to house their educational dramatics in comparative splendour. A new trend is, in consequence, beginning. Managements are now organizing professional companies and booking them for tours of college theatres in 'attractions' which they can persuade college authorities to accept as educational. It seems to me an excellent idea. The colleges at last begin to see on campus some performances of professional standards, so far not always at the highest level, but likely to improve as the idea catches on: the theatrical managements have some incentive to produce more serious stuff; the actors play in better-equipped houses and meet better-educated more discriminating audiences. It is an admirable and practical means of bridging the gulf of mutual suspicion and jealousy which has for so many years divided the professional from the academic theatre.

### Curriculum

Most of the dramatic schools which I know seem to me to spend too much time on classes planned to stimulate the imagination of the students – 'inspirational' classes.

If a student has very little imagination, he ought not, in my view, to be encouraged towards the stage. On the other hand, many students of lively imagination need encouragement to express themselves with confidence and some training in disciplining their imaginations. But I notice that most beginners find it difficult to express their imaginative ideas, not because they need encouragement, but because they lack technique. An imaginative young man does not find it too difficult to put himself imaginatively into the place of Hamlet and he does not find the soliloquies either imaginatively, or even syntactically, beyond his grasp. Where all but a very few are entirely baffled is that they lack, and know that they lack, the skill to make the soliloquies interesting; often they can't even make them intelligible.

I believe, therefore, that a student at drama school should spend at least 60 per cent of his first year on the study of the voice. This is entirely contrary to the practice of any schools which I know. For example, at least three dramatic departments in large and reputable American colleges either offer no voice lessons at all, or else allot to them a negligible amount of time. In none of the three is there a voice-coach attached to the drama department. In one of them, where the department has a staff of ten, over and above graduates giving some part-time instruction, the students go once a week for voice lessons to one of the singing coaches of the music department. The class which I attended lasted for an hour, and there were about twenty-five students. It was clearly impossible for the teacher to give more than the sketchiest attention to individuals. He made an attempt to deal with the situation by very sensibly making the students do breathing exercises and utter vocal sounds – 'O', 'OO', 'AH', 'EH', and so on – aiming to achieve a choral crescendo and diminuendo, with a view to suggesting the principles of breath control. Most of the class were politely, but unmistakably bored, and, when I questioned them later, could see in these classes no relevance whatsoever to acting or drama. 'We don't figure to be singers,' one of them said, 'I haven't got A Voice.' It did not occur to him that without a voice, he would not be able to speak, let alone act. And, indeed, I think that there is a fairly general, if not always conscious, distinction made between a voice, which is a practical mechanism for vocal communication on a utilitarian level ('Pass the mustard' or 'Do you stock them in size ten?') and, on the other hand, A Voice, which if you develop it in an extremely artificial manner, preferably in Italy or Germany, enables you to sing.

I would have thought that one of the first lessons which a drama student must learn is not only that he has a voice, but that his voice is infinitely the most important tool of his trade, on the mastery of which depends the success of his career. You might suppose that this is such a truism that there is no point in even mentioning it. But, in fact, nearly every student and, to be honest, nearly every manager or agent, thinks that the voice is entirely secondary, that the important thing for the actor is Personality.

Well, so, in a sense, it is. The mistake, I suggest, is to think that the voice is not the most distinctive element in an actor's personality, unless we happen to be considering silent movies. But right now far more importance is attached to how actors look than how they sound.

It is perfectly true that appearance is an extremely important factor. But appearance is so very much a matter of make-up, arrangement of the hair, of tailoring, and, above all, of self-confidence. Good looks, to an immense extent, can be achieved by careful study, by drawing attention away from bad points and emphasizing good ones. This is a well-known fact and practically everyone takes this sort of care over their appearance. But hardly anyone takes similar care over what they sound like. Moreover, the amount of fakery, as opposed to real cultivation, which can be applied to the voice is extremely limited. You cannot improve a voice by the simple cosmetic aids which improve a complexion.

Young actors do well to search for personality, but they do not always search in the right place. Here is a field in which drama schools could offer sounder advice than they usually do. They should stress that an expressive voice is an element of personality every bit as important as a pair of good legs or brilliant eyes; that a dull or raucous or weak voice is a far greater drawback than thick ankles or a flat chest.

However, to be just, 'personality' is not stressed by academic theatre so heavily as 'imagination'. Heroic efforts are made to 'liberate' the imagination of students. Departments of theatre are usually attached to what are called Colleges of Liberal Arts. One of the features of Liberal Arts seems to be that you learn about your subject theoretically but practice is not highly regarded. The aim is to create 'well-rounded personalities' rather than mere technicians. It is a little like the eighteenth-century surgeon who certainly studied anatomy but, when it came to the physical work of amputation, he merely supervised the barber. Too many students, by the time they achieve a degree in drama, are stuffed to the gills with theory, have imaginations which are theoretically 'liberated', but which are, in fact, fettered because of their almost total lack of practical know-how, especially in the all-important field of vocal technique.

The reason that voice-training is so neglected is that its value has been underestimated not merely by students, or by the heads of drama schools, but by the general public and, in particular, by the governing bodies of schools and colleges and by ministers and ministries of education. Right now, if a particular school were to install an absolutely first-class vocal coach, the appointment would be of no general interest whatsoever. It would enhance the school's prestige rather less than the appointment of a new janitor or accountant, infinitely less than the appointment of a coach to the football team.

Demand is low and therefore so is supply. It's extremely hard to find, not merely a first-class vocal coach, but even a fourth-class one, who isn't a perfect ninny or a pretentious fake. And, of course, this is just beginning to be a splendid field for pretentious fakes. American education – that gigantic abstraction which, like God, moves in a mysterious way – is just beginning to be dimly aware that vocal training is a gaping hole in the fabric of its curriculum. Over the next few years there will be a hue and cry for voice teachers. Since hardly anyone from the heads of drama departments down – and up – is qualified to judge whether a voice teacher does, or doesn't know his business, some strange appointments will be made. And this state of affairs will continue until, and unless, the training of 'the speaking voice' once more begins to be tackled not only seriously but intelligently, until more people can tell a well-used from a misused voice.

Back to curriculum: in practice I would insist that before the end of his first term a student of acting should have mastered the phonetic symbols and have a working knowledge of phonetics, involving, as it does, the development of a capacity to listen very acutely, and to criticize the sound of the spoken word apart from its content. Learning the elements of phonetics is quite a bore, but no more so than learning to read or write. It is far less of a drudgery than taking the first steps towards playing the 'cello; and far less of an affliction to friends and well-wishers.

Before the end of his first year in school, a student should be required to pass a simple exam on the anatomy of the vocal mechanism. He should also have to pass tests in breath-control and enunciation. Finally, I should insist that he be able to sight-read a vocal line and be able to 'stick to his part' in a concerted piece of not too difficult harmony and counter-point – Handel, say, as opposed to Schönberg.

If he could not pass these tests, I should sling him out, well aware that one might be tipping out John Barrymore with the bathwater. But a good dramatic school ought not to exist for the one or two 'stars' which it may turn out in a decade. They certainly are in-valuable advertisements, but, for the discriminating, a better advertisement is the general level of student achievement. This level, I have noticed over and over again, is always being dragged down by lazy and undisciplined nuisances who get away with murder because they *look* like potential 'star material'.

You will have observed that the above tests are primarily musical. But so is acting, and I believe that the principal shortcoming in the training of actors today is that the connection with music has been almost entirely set aside in favour of amateur psycho-analysis. Even the so-called plastic aspects of the actors's craft – gesture, fencing, stage-falls and so on – all demand musicality. If the beginner learns something of these in his first year, that is fine. There is, after all, a limit to the time during which you can grind the nose of an ardent, high-spirited young person upon the phonetic alphabet.

In most schools, however, beginners spend quite an amount of their time already rehearsing whole plays, or scenes from plays. This, I suggest, is asking them to run before they can even creep. For the most part, they perform the plays so execrably that the effort is all but pointless, as well as being horribly discouraging to all concerned.

## Improvisation

When they aren't getting up plays, beginners, I find, spend a good deal of time and effort on an activity called Improvisation.

I cannot see of what use this is to an actor. My experience of improvisation is rather limited, but I can appreciate at once that it could be valuable in the training of a journalist or a novelist or to the writer of advertising copy. It demands that you are quick and flexible in your reaction to what your partners in the 'improv' are up to: you must be witty and poignant, as occasion demands in the verbal exchanges, inventive in the situations, able to see whither a word or an action may lead. What has any of this to do with the actor? He is not going to be called upon to make up plots and situations and lines to express them; nor to invent off the cuff, but rather, by means of the very gradual process of rehearsal, to search for the clearest, wittiest, most interesting or most moving way to express the invention of someone else.

I am reluctant to decry improvisation, because it is a method dear to the heart of several directors whose work I admire and whose good sense I respect, Peter Brook especially. I can imagine certain situations where the actors and their director are stumped as to the meaning of a scene. They agree to try to find the elusive meaning by 'improvising' an analogous situation. I still think that this is a literary, rather than histrionic exercise. But let that pass. Many actors are literate, though I must say that most of those whom I have greatly admired are neither very literate nor very good at off-the-cuff invention. The literate types, who excel at charades, are usually hams. If, however, an improvised analogy is to be helpful it must be executed, I would have thought, with a skill and authority far beyond the capacity of beginners. What I cannot see is why improvisation should be considered a valuable part of elementary training.

There is another form of improvisation as well as the kind in which a group invents a concerted scene: it is the kind where a single performer is asked to express himself in a given situation. This is obviously easier – no reaction to, or from, other performers, possibly no dialogue – and I can see that improvisations of this kind may be valuable as a very elementary lesson in performing without self-consciousness. Further, such improvisations can teach the beginner that he must direct the focus of the audience's attention, and that, therefore, there must be absolutely no irrelevant movements or ideas. These are valuable lessons. All performers have to learn them at some stage. But I should have thought the time and place

1 Adelaide Ristori (1822–1906) as Maria Stuart. Shaw regarded Ristori, together with Duse, ▶
Coquelin and Salvini, as the greatest actors whom he had seen.

2 Tommaso Salvini (1830–191?)
as Othello

3 Benoît Constant Coquelin (1841–1909)

4 Sarah Bernhardt (1844–
1923) as Theodora

5 Sarah Bernhardt shortly
before her death in 1923

6  Eleanora Duse

7  Eleanora Duse (1859–1924)

8  Maurice Evans as Hamlet at the Old Vic 1936

9  Katharine Cornell as Elizabeth Barrett
in *The Barretts of Wimpole Street*,
New York 1931

10   George Robey as Mrs Crusoe in *Robinson Crusoe*, Bristol 1942

11   The Music Hall artist Vesta Tilley performing *The Midnight Sun* c. 1900

12 The Lunts (Lynn Fontanne and Alfred Lunt) in *The Taming of the Shrew*, New York 1935

13  Lilian Gish as Ophelia and Judith Anderson as the Queen in *Hamlet*, New York 1936

14  Edith Evans and Ruth Gordon in *The Country Wife*, Old Vic Company 1936

15  John Barrymore as Hamlet, London 1925

16  Helen Hayes as Victoria Regina 1935; an actress of great charm and ability whose quality has never been tested in great roles

17  Charles Laughton, the most impressive character actor of his generation, in Josef von Sternberg's film *I, Claudius* 1937

18  John Gielgud as Hamlet, New Theatre 1934

19  Laurence Olivier as Caesar in
*Caesar and Cleopatra*, St James's
Theatre, London 1951

20 Laurence Olivier as Becket, St James's Theatre, New York 1960

21 Laurence Olivier as Archie Rice in *The Entertainer*, English Stage Company 1957

23 Sybil Thorndike as Jocasta and Laurence Olivier as Oedipus in *Oedipus*, Old Vic Company 1945; the two actors with the most impressive range among their contemporaries

22 Laurence Olivier as Astrov in *Uncle Vanya*, Chichester Festival Theatre Company 1962

24  Sybil Thorndike as Aase in *Peer Gynt*, Old Vic Company 1944

25  Sybil Thorndike as Mrs
    Railton-Bell in *Separate
    Tables*, Australia 1955

26  Sybil Thorndike as
    Marina with George
    Relph as Telyegin in
    *Uncle Vanya*, Old Vic
    Company 1945

29  David Warner as Hamlet, Royal Shakespeare Company, Stratford-upon-Avon 1965

Drama schools in action

27  Judith Bellis and Aaron Silver in RADA's Vanbrugh Theatre production of *The Lark* 1969

28  LAMDA production of *The Feast* (based on *The Satyricon*) 1969

30  William Hutt as Tartuffe and Angela Wood as Elmire in *Tartuffe*,
    Stratford Shakespearean Festival Theatre, Ontario 1969

31 Jean-Louis Barrault as M. Bérenger and Dominique Arden as Martha in *Le Piéton de l'Air*, Théâtre de France 1965

32  *The Frogs*, The Greek Art Theatre 1967

33 *Frankenstein*, The Living Theatre 1969

34  Sabin Epstein, Lon Zeldis and Patrick Burke in Café La Mama production of
*Arden of Faversham* 1970

35  *US*, Royal Shakespeare Company, Aldwych 1966

36  Dancers' Workshop 'Myth' *Carry*

37  Maggie Smith as Hedda and Robert Stephens as Ejlert Lövborg in *Hedda Gabler*, National Theatre Company 1970

38  George Baker as The Son and Peggy Ashcroft as The Mother in *Days in the Trees*,
Royal Shakespeare Company, Aldwych 1966

39  Martin Held as Krapp in *Krapp's Last Tape*, Schiller Theater 1970

40  Richard Kay as Phoebe and Ronald Pickup as Rosalind in the all-male production of
*As You Like It*, National Theatre Company 1967

was the classroom at a tender age; such elements should have been thoroughly mastered before the stage of a university acting course, let alone a professional acting school.

Can it be that improvisation is so stressed because of economic convenience? It's so nice and cheap. No books to buy, no royalties to pay, no scenery, no props, no time spent on the drudgery of learning lines. One can get through at least eight or ten 'improvs' in the course of a single class. In an hour eight or ten students can be given the chance to show what they can do, can be for a few moments the centre of attraction. And, from the teacher's point of view they are lovely and easy to arrange: no need to read a text beforehand, with the attendant bother of having to wonder what the damn thing's trying to say. All you need to do is to set a subject, let the performers loose upon it, then give a few words of encouraging criticism.

I would very respectfully suggest to drama teachers that, in place of improvisation, they should seriously consider rehearsed readings of plays. As with improvisation, readings would not involve the fuss and expense of production. They would, however, be useful illustration and expansion of the vocal classes. Under direction the students would learn what it means to shape their phrases and to vary their length. They would learn the important and, though easily apprehensible, almost entirely neglected, technique of giving and taking cues, so that each actor's performance dovetails into a musical ensemble. Finally, by reading them together, they would get a valuable first impression of many important plays.

### Make-up and movement

Classes in make-up will not come amiss. But the limits of what can be learnt and taught are rather soon reached. Most of the so-called experts in make-up are nothing of the kind. They are people who have had a few lessons, know some of the technical elements of how to apply make-up, of shading and high-lighting. Few of them have any ideas beyond one or two rules of thumb. These they pass on and it is as well for acting students to learn them. But I cannot feel that learning the technique of applying make-up is as important as having the taste and imagination to apply it appropriately and judiciously. This can partly be taught and learnt in school, but only partly. Make-up, in my opinion, should form part of general instruction in Learning to See, in looking at paintings, sculpture, advertisements, landscapes, flowers, animals, people and machinery; and in being able to discuss what you see and fail to see. There is a tendency in all the education with which I have been connected to assume that because most of us can see, we do see. Quite a grave misconception. In general we only see what we already know to be there. A botanist will see in a ditch fifteen or twenty different plants, where the non-botanist will be aware of no more than an undifferentiated mass of greenery. Many of us could see a great deal more than we do if we were intelligently guided and encouraged.

Classes in movement are customary in dramatic schools and are doubtless of value. It is important that an actor should be in good muscular trim and should have a good physical posture and co-ordination. All this can be considerably developed in class, as can physical, and thence to some important extent, spiritual relaxation. On the whole the need is well understood for instruction in movement, with appropriate emphasis on dancing, fencing, falls, and so on. I think, perhaps, more attention could be given to such extremely simple elements as walking, running, sitting down, so as to make these actions not merely practical but expressive. And, again, students should be encouraged to *observe* movement. Watch a cat preparing to jump; a dog making itself comfortable in its basket; a nervous lady at a supermarket; a stockbroker getting into his car; observe how old people *really* move, as opposed to the stereotype of old, which actors are wont to trot out as realistic.

*Drama is not literature*

Just as improvisation is an economically convenient way to teach acting, so is it economically convenient to pretend that drama is literature and can be adequately studied as part of a literary curriculum. Students are encouraged to believe that they can, as part of a training in English literature, 'do' Shakespeare, Jonson, Congreve, Sheridan, Shaw and a sprinkling of foreign drama in translation. This is analogous to encouraging them to believe that they can 'do' surgery by taking a general course in biology.

In the present climate of public opinion there are virtually limitless funds available for lunar exploration or medical research; whereas the funds available for the study of literature are relatively scanty and for that of drama, *per se*, non-existent. Very good. The objectionable thing is not the lack of funds, not even the pretence by authority that funds cannot be found (they could be tomorrow if the study of drama were thought to be – and I am not suggesting that it is – as useful as the study of the common cold). The objectionable thing is the complacent hypocrisy which pretends that drama can be adequately studied as literature, adequately taught by literary professors.

We can see how this comes about. It so happens that a certain number of the very greatest expressions of the human spirit are in dramatic form – *The Oresteia, Oedipus Rex, Hamlet, Phèdre, Faust, Peer Gynt, Saint Joan*, to quote a few examples. Their texts, however, though dramatic, are accessible in printed form, that is to say in a similar form to the texts of masterpieces of another kind – *The Faerie Queene, Paradise Lost* or *Endymion;* or of yet another kind, *Pilgrim's Progress, David Copperfield* or *Huckleberry Finn*. This gives colour to the argument that dramatic masterpieces can be studied as literature, because it certainly is possible to read them. And the argument – compelling enough in present circumstances – is that they must be studied as literature or not at all.

Now a musical score is *not* accessible to any and every reader; to decipher a full orchestral score is a very specialized and rare accomplishment. Is it only on this account that the symphonies of Beethoven are not, by the application of the same argument which applies to drama, studied as literature?

Or, putting the argument another way round: why is Kant's *Critique of Pure Reason* not studied as literature? The answer, in this case, is that in the mid-Victorian translation still current it is virtually unreadable. Indispensable to the philosopher, it is a literary monster. Can it be that drama 'counts' as literature because it is not only accessible in print but enjoyable? But is that a reason for neglecting its study in the form which the author intended?

Of course, I agree that drama *can* be studied as literature and that such studies can be valuable. The mere textual elucidation is so; as well as a great deal of work which has to be done, and will continue, on the explication of ideas and characters. I certainly would not like to devalue the immense debt which the theatre, in this respect, owes to scholarship. What is objectionable is the belief that this sort of study suffices.

Does it?

How many students really get, from their studies of drama as a part of English Literature, the idea that only some, and by no means always the most significant, aspects of a great play reveal themselves to a reader?

How far can they apprehend that drama is a musical and pictorial expression, as well as literary? Often there are whole passages where either music, or spectacle, or both, are actually more important than the meaning of the words. Music, by the way, in this context, does not mean the introduction of formal musical effects into the text – a song, trumpet calls, processional marches and so on – but rather the music of the spoken word, the musical aspect of the text.

How many literary students realize that the scenes in a well-written play are 'built up' by means of musical patterns, created by the actors' voices? A well-written climax is engineered on a plan analogous to the kind of *stretto* which Rossini uses in opera, or Beethoven in a symphony, to achieve a climax.

How many literary students realize that a great dramatic soliloquy is an 'aria', in which the breathing, the tempo, the pauses, the emphases have to be planned?

Why, you may ask, need students know about matters of technique which are relevant only for the actor?

The answer is that the 'meaning' of a speech is not solely a matter of apprehending its grammar and syntax. It is equally, and sometimes more importantly, a matter of apprehending its purely musical content.

Take, for example, two soliloquies of Hamlet: 'To be or not to be' and 'O, what a rogue and peasant slave'. The first is much the easier as well as much the shorter. A student, merely by reading it, can get an immediate grasp of its not very profound philosophy, and can infer its quiet, reflective tone. A well-graced actor may be able to illuminate this aspect or that, but, on the whole, acting does not make it so much more lively than it already is to an intelligent reader.

But now take 'O, what a rogue and peasant slave'. To begin with it is doubtful if most readers will fully realize the power of the musical and pictorial effect which introduces it. The stage has been full – Players, Courtiers, Hamlet, Horatio, Polonius – the scene with the players has been full of bustle and animation. Hamlet dismisses them all politely and unmistakably. In a matter of seconds, the stage is empty. Hamlet stands by himself before the audience – 'Now I am alone'.

There then follows a highly confidential, emotional outpouring. This will be intelligible enough to a reader. But will the ordinary reader appreciate that the speech has three strongly contrasted moods, three musical 'movements'?

The first is a steady build-up of anger and self-contempt leading to 'O, vengeance!' This is followed by a reaction, an anti-climax: 'Why, what an ass am I!' Then the second movement begins: 'About, my brain! I have heard that guilty creatures sitting at a play...' whereupon he starts with characteristic intensity and energy to plan the Mousetrap. This idea or movement also builds to a climax: 'I know my course.' But then, again characteristically, doubt supervenes: 'the spirit that I have seen may be the devil'. This doubt and fear again works to a peak, the shortest climax of the three, and though less noisy and ranting than the first, it is the most intense, nearest to the matter. 'The devil ... abuses me to damn me.' A pause. Then the moment of decision (I cannot understand the critics who maintain that Hamlet is an indecisive character, this is only one of many instances where his will closes on a problem with a completely decisive snap): 'I'll have grounds more relative than this' – that is to say proof more conclusive than the dubious accusations of a midnight spectre – 'The play's the thing wherein I'll catch the conscience of the king.'

Now it may be that nine students of literature out of ten could offer a musical analysis of this speech at least as good as the foregoing. I doubt it. I have heard too many of them try, and fail, to read aloud with even the smallest awareness that the speech is a piece of music.

If it is not easy for a literary student (or for that matter, professor) to grasp the music of a soliloquy, how much harder is it to 'hear' the music of an ensemble, where the dramatic effect largely depends upon the contrast in tone, pitch, pace and, of course, intention, between one voice and another; where this purely musical contrast is every bit as meaningful as the actual words which each character utters.

Take, for example, the scandal scenes in Sheridan's *School for Scandal*, where the speakers outdo one another in witty malice; or take the scene in *Henry VIII* (Act III, sc. 2) where my Lords Norfolk, Suffolk, Surrey and the Lord Chamberlain combine to bait the Cardinal. It would have been possible for the purpose of this scene to roll these four characters into one, with small loss, even possibly gain, to a reader; but as an ensemble, a quartet of accusers, it is musically and choreographically incomparably more powerful and interesting.

One more point: how many literary instructors are aware that in Shakespeare the key moments, the moments of principal dramatic consequence, are quite often not 'in the lines' at all? A study of the lines will not reveal them. They occur, like most theatrical key-moments, in silence, during a pause.

Two instances will suffice, I hope, to clinch this point.

The first is from the fifth (and last) act of *The Tempest*. 'Now,' says Prospero, 'does my project gather to a head.' His project is revenge. And Prospero's long-meditated vengeance upon his usurping brother is now beginning to go great guns. The low people, the greedy and untrustworthy servants, are already in bad trouble. Prospero has charged his goblins that they crack their joints with dry convulsions, shorten up their sinews with aged cramps and more pinch-spotted make them than pard or cat-o'-mountain. Their screams can be heard. Prospero feels no pity: 'Let them be hunted soundly', is his comment, 'At this hour, lie at my mercy all mine enemies . . .' and then a moment later says to Ariel: 'Say, my spirit, how fares the King and 's followers?' Ariel then describes their case, which is anything but agreeable. 'Your charm so strongly works 'em,' says Ariel, after describing their misery, 'that if you beheld them, your affections would become tender.'

*Prospero*　Dost thou think so, Spirit?

*Ariel*　Mine would, sir, were I human.

*Prospero*　And mine shall.

This is the crisis of the play. From now on *The Tempest* is succeeded by a golden evening's calm of forgiveness and reconciliation. But nothing in the text marks this. The actors and their director are left to search and find the way without signposts. I find it hard to credit that a reader, unaided, will apprehend that this is the play's turning-point, a great and intensely moving moment. And, even if he is intellectually aware of this, I doubt whether he would have the slightest idea of the technical means to make it clear.

The moment can be interpreted in many ways; but whichever way may be chosen, the two actors must be directed to mark it in the most significant possible manner.

I suggest that Prospero should pause after Ariel says '. . . your affections would become tender' and before he says, 'Dost thou think so, Spirit?' in order to indicate that, suddenly, unexpectedly it has occurred to him, obsessed as he has been with the idea of revenge, that there is an alternative; that mercy may conceivably be a better idea than vengeance or justice.

Then Ariel replies: 'Mine would, sir. . . .' And remember that Shakespeare has, a few lines previously, reminded us that Ariel is a captive spirit, Prospero's slave, a sub-human agent to the powerful magician. A few lines back the sub-human has been begging for liberty. The full speech now is: 'Mine would, sir, *were I human.*'

This would work, I suggest, as a stabbing reminder to Prospero that power carries with it responsibility; responsibility not only to slaves but to enemies. Another pause is called for, this time far more emotional. After the pause, the deeply moved reply: 'And mine shall.' Thus might the whole change of heart be clearly intelligible.

I am not for a moment suggesting that the foregoing is the 'right' way to mark the significance of the moment, merely that it is one possible way. But marked the moment must be, and I have the gravest doubts that one theatrically inexperienced reader in a thousand would even perceive that it is a crisis, let alone have the very least idea of how, technically, to express it.

Another instance of a key moment, which is not in the lines at all, and is therefore likely to escape the notice of a reader: in the great finale of *Measure for Measure* the Duke, a figurative presentation of omnipotence and, therefore, I think, a figure of God, has made an unexpected re-entry into his city (called in the play Vienna, but clearly again a figurative presentation of any and every city) to restore order and justice to the capital. Angelo, his corrupt deputy, is sentenced to death. Mariana, now Angelo's wife, begs the Duke to spare him. Her plea is getting nowhere and she implores Isabella, who stands high in the Duke's favour, to kneel by her side and lend weight to her prayer. Isabella has the greatest reason to hate Angelo and approve of his punishment.

In a torrent of emotion, Mariana throws herself at the feet of the Duke and cries:

> 'O my good Lord! Sweet Isabel take my part
> Lend me your knees, and all my life to come
> I'll lend you all my life to do you service.

*Duke*    Against all sense you do importune her:
> Should she kneel down in mercy of this fact,
> Her brother's ghost his paved bed would break,
> And take her hence in horror.

*Mariana*    Sweet Isabel, do yet but kneel by me; Isabel,
> Hold up your hands, say nothing; I'll speak all . . .
> O Isabel, will you not lend a knee?

Then, just as Isabella is moving to kneel beside Mariana, the Duke reminds her:

*Duke*    He dies for Claudio's death.

That is to say, Angelo is about to be justly executed for the unjust execution of Isabella's greatly-loved brother. There is a pause. Like Prospero, Isabella weighs justice against mercy. The scale dips in favour of mercy. She kneels.

In the hurly-burly of one of Shakespeare's most tumultuous and elaborate scenes it is all too easy for a reader to pass this by and, in missing Isabella's silent gesture of forgiveness, to miss a great moment, not only touching in itself, but one which indicates that Shakespeare has made the play something much more serious than its complicated, romantic plot. It is an allegory of the contrast between power used selfishly and irresponsibly and power used justly and mercifully. This moment is a statement of the Mercy Theme, the more powerful because the pause changes the music of the scene. It has been going hell for leather; Mariana's hysterical pleas and the Duke's implacable replies are long and repetitious, unless propelled as forcefully and fast as two good actors can achieve. The sudden silence of the pause, the slow deliberate rhythm of Isabella's kneeling, make a most striking musical contrast with what has gone before.

Reading the play to oneself, with the necessary concentration upon meaning not upon music, is absolutely not the way to achieve the effects of orchestration, but without these, meaning can be only partially and feebly realized. Meaning, in short, is, in drama, only partly literary. The total meaning of a play includes sight and sound, not merely the intellectual apprehension of the symbols on a printed page.

Breathes there the literary student of Shakespeare, who is not familiar with Theobald's inspired emendation in Mrs Quickly's description of Falstaff's death. The unintelligible phrase 'a table of green fields' is emended to 'a babbled of green fields'. This is a fascinating and justly celebrated piece of textual scholarship and, *for a reader*, makes intelligible an otherwise unintelligible phrase. But, *for an actress*, it really makes little difference. Her business is to move and interest the audience by her (Mrs Quickly's) characteristic description of the old man's death. She has to give a *general* impression, from which a garbled version of one phrase, describing one particular fact (and not necessarily the most important: to my mind the facts that his nose was sharp as a pen, and the fumbling with the bedclothes and the turning of the tide are every bit as touching and meaningful as his babbling of green fields) really makes no difference at all to the way she plays the scene, or the impression it makes upon the audience.

How many students of literature have it pointed out to them that in many scenes the text is simply a reach-me-down accompaniment to spectacle and action. In the opening scene of *The Tempest*, for example, the lines between Boatswain and Master merely indicate the bustle and panic of a shipwreck; Henry V's 'Once more unto the breach' is no more than a long and supremely eloquent trumpet blast, the 'scoring' is *intended* to outweigh any literary meaning.

Perhaps I have laboured at too great length the inadequacy of studying drama as literature. I do so because this method of study is still almost universally accepted as right and reasonable. I want to suggest that it is not right and not reasonable and that it prevails simply because it is economically convenient. It is cheaper to regard drama as a rather stagnant tributary of the mainstream of literature. This shabby fact is rationalized and regarded as respectable, not just in educational establishments of the highest reputation but by Boards of Regents and Governors right up to the level of National Ministries.

# 4 *Actor and director*

Since I suppose that many of those who will read this book are likely to be actors or students of acting or amateur actors, I shall now offer a few 'tips' about the actor's relation to his director.

Time was when, in the production of a play, there was no one whose duties corresponded with those of the present-day director, or producer. (In Britain it is customary to refer to the producer; whereas in America the same person is called the director. The producer in America is responsible for finance and administration and is, in Britain, called the manager.)

Formerly the director's function was fulfilled by the actor-manager (Henry Irving, for instance, directed his own productions at the Lyceum Theatre in London for more than twenty years, 1878–1901), by the author or, perhaps most frequently, by the manager, a theatrical businessman.

Always, however, there has to be somebody in charge of the rehearsals of a play, just as, unless anarchy is to prevail, there has to be someone in charge of any co-operative activity. At rehearsals someone must act as chairman of the proceedings, to arbitrate conflicting interests, to unify conflicting ideas of interpretation, even to initiate ideas. In the interests of efficiency this person must at rehearsal be accorded the same sort of authority which is accorded to the chairman of a business or political meeting.

It is a myth, widely believed and expressed in almost all films and novels about the theatre, that rehearsals take place in a tumult of what is called temperament. 'Artists' are represented as screaming, tearing up their parts and their clothes, stamping out and slamming the doors, slapping one another in the face and telephoning their lawyers. And, of course, in such fictions it is almost obligatory that, on the eve of what is called the Première, the leading lady shall fall ill, or be detained by a snow-storm in Chicago or a motor smash at Pangbourne. The understudy cannot leave her mother's death-bed; the understudy's understudy (there are such things) is drunk.

'What is to be done?' cries the distracted director. Directors in such stories are invariably
distracted. 'Who knows the part?'
'I do, sir,' falters little Mary Dewdrop.
'You, Mary?' cries the director, 'Why you're only – only . . .'
'It's true, sir. Only a dresser, but I know the rôle. I used to "hear" Madam every night.'

Well, naturally, she goes 'on' and sails triumphantly through without the smallest hesitation.

Everyone sits up all night till 'the papers' come out – another invariable rule in this kind of fiction.

The critics, one and all, declare that Mary Dewdrop is Rachel, Bernhardt, Duse and Mrs Fiske rolled into one. By lunchtime she is world-famous. By nightfall she is in Hollywood, appearing on television in her own serial, entitled *Mary Makes Good*.

In fact, in a very long experience, involving countless emergencies, I have never known an understudy to go on and be more than passable: a pale dim shadow of his or her principal. At the end, if he has managed to get through the performance without total disaster, everyone crowds round and offers sincerely grateful congratulations, because the day has been saved. But they all know, and later on in a calmer moment, the understudy will know too, that, in fact, the performance was no damn good and couldn't possibly be any good. It simply isn't possible to go on at short notice and be good in a large part in which you have had skimpy rehearsals in a production designed to fit somebody else, whose personality, as well as whose clothes, you are called upon to assume in exceedingly flustering circumstances.

I have described such an emergency at some length simply to stress the wide gap between theatrical fiction and fact.

Rehearsals do NOT occur in a tumult of temperament. Actors are, with soldiers and sailors, the best disciplined of any kind of workers, and for the same reason: they all know that the punishments for indiscipline are extremely severe, that the ultimate sanction is death. Naturally I do not mean that management has power to hang, behead, shoot or even electrocute an unruly mummer. But the profession is so crowded that no one, literally no one, dare be A Serious Nuisance.

If you are a serious nuisance it soon gets around. No management will hire you. When there are ten, twenty, maybe a hundred applicants waiting for every job, management can afford to pick and choose. The sanction, which ensures good discipline among actors, is not entirely their splendid character and dedication, it is also connected with the law of supply and demand.

As a teacher in an excellent English boarding school I beheld in three brief terms more tantrums in the staff common-room, more stamping and pouting and squealing and rushing from the room in tears of temper than I have encountered in almost fifty years of theatrical rehearsal. This is because schoolmasters, like clergymen, plumbers and home helps, operate in a field where demand exceeds supply.

If, in real life, a theatrical director is 'distracted', the cause is quite unlikely to be the difficulty of getting his cast to attend to business. Professional discipline ensures that they will accord to him at least an outward semblance of respect and attention. His distraction is more likely to be the result of knowing that at least half his cast knows more about acting in general than he does himself, and that, in particular, their interpretation of whatever play is being prepared is likely to be very much better than his own.

Nevertheless, every actor must make it his business to co-operate with his director. This is merely to avoid anarchy. It does not mean blind obedience; nor does it mean that the actor should surrender his own opinion. It may, however, sometimes be wiser and easier to do so.

Inevitably directors vary. Some demand, may even deserve, a more unquestioning obedience than others. Some make too few demands, are too timid or too lazy to take the lead which it is their duty to take.

Since this book is about acting, not directing, let me say, from a director's point of view, formed over a long experience, what I hope for from an actor. Absolutely I do *not* want him to concede that, by virtue of my office, I am always right. That would be absurd. But I do hope that he will concede me the right sometimes to be wrong; that if my point of view of a play or even of the actor's own part differs from his, then, if after reasonable argument we can reach no agreement, he must either play the part as directed, or play it in his way in another production. But, this once granted, I expect the actor to feel completely free to make suggestions, to try experiments, to discuss, to argue, provided that all this does not (in my opinion) take up too much of everyone's time at rehearsal; also provided that his suggestions and experiments do not conflict with the interests of other actors.

I certainly do not expect to coach or to teach actors to play their parts. It would obviously be wild if I were to give lessons to Maggie Smith on how to make a line sound witty, or to suggest inflections to Sir John Gielgud.

But I do feel entitled to offer, even to persons no less experienced and far more talented than myself, suggestions which they are at liberty to take or reject. I regard our relation as being like that of an editor to an experienced writer. The more experienced, self-confident writers welcome editorial suggestions, provided that they are reasonably intelligent and entirely disinterested. I try my best to ensure that my directorial suggestions to experienced actors are so.

Less experienced actors may reasonably expect rather more suggestions but also may reasonably resent them, if they imply lack of intelligence on my part or theirs, or lack of technical capacity. In return for their co-operation, actors have a right to expect of any director the good manners and consideration which are due to any group of colleagues from its leader, chairman, foreman, gaffer, or whatever the term may be.

If a director expects actors to be punctual, he cannot ever be late. If he expects their concentration, he must not only concentrate, but must be seen to concentrate at every second of every minute of rehearsal.

If your director singles you out, this does not necessarily imply either praise or blame. It is more likely for the purpose of experiment, to try a different emphasis or a different choreographic arrangement, to suggest another angle on a character or a situation. The experiment may not, quite probably will not, be any better than what you were doing. But then again, it may be; and only by experiment can best results be had. Actors are apt to be self-conscious when one of their 'moments' becomes the subject of experiment.

Contrariwise, don't feel, if none of your scenes are subjects of experiment, that this is because the director considers that you – and the scenes – are a dead loss. I am always being taken aside by actors who say: 'You have something to say to everyone except me. Is it because I'm so dreadfully bad?' I try to assure them that, if I thought their scenes were bad I should be trying hard to get them better; that, if they aren't worked over and over, this means that, to my mind at all events, they are in good shape.

Don't be afraid to speak to the director and make suggestions: 'Will you, please, try this scene in such a way? May I make the exit more slowly? Need I stammer? Must I wear brown shoes?' Even if your suggestions aren't accepted you'll almost certainly find out the idea behind the rapid exit or the brown shoes. Just possibly it may be a sound idea.

The director has the right to suggest ideas to you. You have a reciprocal right, only you should exercise it in private and your suggestions must only concern your own part. It is not in order to request the director to tell another actor not to wear blue, because you think blue doesn't 'go' with your dress. It is in order to ask him to request the other actor not to blow his nose just when you are trying to say the best line in your part. It's in order; but it may not be very wise. It might be better just to shout the line.

# 5   *What is good acting?*

*Wide range*

It is only theoretically possible to separate the actor's skill from his personality. Theoretically, however, there is a difference. I suppose the skill of acting lies largely in the fact that the performer is able to suppress certain traits of his personality and to emphasize others, to get the results that he wants. Theoretically, then, the most skilful actor should be the most protean, the actor with the widest range.

It so happens, however, that the actors with the widest range do not usually go very deep. I have known many protean actors who could achieve startling changes in their appearance, voice and mannerisms, but their performances were apt to be superficial.

In the palmy days of vaudeville there used to be protean or quick-change acts. The artist would come on stage looking like a beggar of a hundred years old; in rags, with quavering voice and tottering gait he would do a brief pathetic sketch. Then the lights would go out, the drums would roll, and when five seconds later there was a cymbal crash and the lights blazed on again, Lo and Behold, the beggar had been replaced by a handsome young buck in top-hat, white tie and tails, who would dance a few elegant steps and sing with assurance and charm. Black-out again, and five seconds later a heavily-built cleaning woman was on her knees, making to scrub the stage, while she recounted the adventures of herself and Mrs 'Arris in the Lamb and Flag last Thursday. Just as she seemed inevitably headed for the bluest of *doubles entendres*, just as the audience began to titter with nervous expectation . . . black-out, and five seconds later a Curate would be discovered in the middle of a Lecture on the Evils of Intemperance.

Such acts were brilliantly skilful, but the performances were mere lightning sketches and I never heard of one of those protean artists being able to give a sustained performance of merit. Similarly, few of the 'straight' actors who excel in a wide range of 'thumbnail sketches' can sustain the long haul of a great play. They are technically adept, but lack the importance of personality, the imaginative insight, which a great part demands.

On the other hand, some of the greatest actors have no protean quality at all. In every part, though the make-up and the costume may vary, the performance is almost exactly the same. John Gielgud is a case in point: matchless in declamation, with extraordinary intelligence, insight and humour, he commands almost no skill as a character actor. Like many other eminent players, he is 'always himself'. Absolutely this is not to derogate the skill, imagination and taste with which such actors 'present' themselves. It is, however, to admit that every artist has his limitations, and to imply that protean range is not the ultimate in theatrical accomplishment.

Of the actors whom I have seen the two who, in my opinion, best combine protean skill with 'star quality' are Laurence Olivier and Sybil Thorndike. Both are more than equal to the long haul and are able, when required, to assume immense nobility, majesty and grandeur. Both excel in the expression of powerful passion. Both can be hilariously funny. Both take almost too much pleasure in the farouche and grotesque, and an endearing, almost childlike delight in looking, sounding and behaving as unlike their 'real selves' as possible.

If only more people had the spiritual freedom, the energy and technical skill to find this sort of release, in escaping their everyday self, there would be many fewer unhappy nuisances plaguing themselves and everyone around them.

## Narrow range

Most people can act reasonably well when the imaginative demands of a part do not exceed their own imaginative experience and when its stylistic demands do not require them to transcend the limits of ordinary behaviour. Of course, this rules out just about all the 'great parts' in which an actor must imagine, speak and move on a heroic scale.

Most actors, however, are content to leave the heroic parts well alone and just to go on and on playing aspects of their own personality, drawing upon their rather limited experience, none of which make exacting, tiresome demands. They believe, quite rightly, that inside narrow limits a great deal of skill can be brought to bear and that talented skilful acting can give interest to quite commonplace material. They are content to develop a high degree of craftsmanship, giving virtually the same highly-polished performance year after respectable and profitable year.

It is not the most ambitious or exciting way to live the life of an actor. But not all actors are ambitious or exciting people. The men and women who live this way are probably taking a very realistic view of their own abilities; and if you like acting, feel you have some talent, but only for small effects, then this is a reasonable and interesting career, in which there is a greater degree of variety, wider range of companionship, more possibilities for travel, than in most other bourgeois occupations. The bourgeois advantages at least balance the bourgeois drawbacks – economic uncertainty, long, irregular hours, and so on.

But most actors, especially in their early days, are more concerned with the romantic possibilities of their calling than with its more bourgeois aspects. They want to 'give people a thrill', as an opera-singer once said to me, when I asked him why he had chosen so risky and exacting a job. Do you agree that the desire is perhaps more generous than merely vain and egotistical? Most of us realize that we may not have what it takes to be a 'great' performer, but we are still anxious to try our wings and at least to be a part, at first, naturally, a very humble and inconspicuous part, of a vividly exciting and influential activity. Gradually most of us begin to find a way towards a sort of life which suits us though this is never quite the fulfilment of the vague, highly-coloured dreams of the romantic beginner.

Beginners necessarily do not know their own potentialities. Those who dream simply of glory, in terms of applause, publicity and huge salaries, hardly ever achieve their ambition, because it is a shallow and selfish one and shallow, selfish people are not the stuff of which greatness is made on the stage, or anywhere else.

## Ups and downs

Beginners have to learn, through a process of timid trial and painful error, what are their strong suits and what their weak. They have to learn that being a good actor is far more than just giving a good performance on the stage. They have to learn to survive. One of the most important survival-techniques in the theatre is not to be unduly puffed up by success, nor cast down by failure. Success and failure have so little to do with one's own effort. You can succeed, very notably, to the extent of laying the foundation for a whole career, if, through sheer luck, you are cast in a successful play and a decent part which exactly suits you; or in a part in which virtually any actor is simply bound to succeed. There are such parts. Saint Joan is one of them; Hamlet is another: Peer Gynt is a third. They exist too in more ephemeral plays. In the 1920s Clemence Dane wrote a successful play called *A Bill of Divorcement*. The leading part not only made the reputation of the young actress who played it (Meggie Albanesi), but whoever played this part – and the play was produced all over the world – if she had any ability at all, succeeded brilliantly. Equally failure, though it may occasionally be one's own fault, is very seldom so.

In any case it is useless to brood on success or failure. This is the curse of the current theatre in New York, where success and failure are still, as everywhere else, largely irrelevant accidents. In New York, however, they cannot be ignored, cannot be taken except with deadly earnestness. The economic effects are too powerful.

On Broadway a youngster of eighteen can be a 'success', however little merited, be wafted overnight to wide celebrity, considerable wealth, and, in every direction, opportunities open up, mostly golden or, at all events, gilded. Conversely, you may be brilliant in a part but the play itself may be a disaster. You are then tarred with the brush of failure. In New York City this is infinitely more repellant than the most disgusting disease. So you will probably be offered no more work for several years; you may never be offered work again.

Every career has its ups and downs. One of the aspects of being a good actor is the ability to handle these ups and downs, to keep your head in a time of great success and to keep your self-confidence in a time of adversity. This means that your life must be based on a sound sense of values.

It is arguable, and very often argued, that such values are harder to maintain in the acting profession than in many others. It is argued that the actor is his own stock-in-trade: his appearance, his sex-appeal, his voice, his emotions are all on offer in the market-place. But, honestly, in a rather more indirect way, so are everyone else's. Is the success of a lawyer, doctor or ecclesiastic entirely detachable from qualities of voice, appearance, humour and so on? What about the salesman and merchant? Are their charms not also on offer? And what about the Great Abstraction of our times The Ordinary Housewife? Does not the success of her career also depend upon self-exploitation?

Actors' values are, I think, vulnerable to the violent fluctuations which beset their economic situation. Values have to be adjusted rather briskly, if on Tuesday you are struggling with debts in a cold-water flat on one meal a day, and the following Friday you find yourself quite affluent, with the totally different anxieties and responsibilities to which affluence is subject. Also these economic fluctuations are usually accompanied by a certain rootlessness. It is rather easy to know where your social duties lie if your entire life is spent as a bank manager, say, or a doctor's wife in a small provincial town, Mullingar, say, or Bismarck, North Dakota. It is a good deal harder if you are whisking about the world in the neighbourless and shifting environment of a touring player. But, by and large, the same basic rules and values apply to all lives. Do unto others . . . and, maybe, the differences in differing circumstances are rather easy to exaggerate.

The best actors, then, are those with sufficient insight to bring to life the dry bones of a text, and sufficient technique to express what they have imagined. Further, they must have sufficient personality to suggest 'greatness'. They must be able, without making fools of themselves, to get up and pretend to be King Oedipus, Hamlet, Macbeth, Rosalind, Phèdre, Faust, Peer Gynt or John Gabriel Borkman. That is to say they must have appearance, stature, intelligence, voice, and, especially, character well over average. Such personality is not simply a gift. Very exceptional young people may have the potentiality for such greatness. But, finally, it is only achieved by long and intense cultivation. One in ten of the potentially great achieve greatness in any field – maybe the figure is one in a hundred. Nine or ninety and nine, fall by the wayside with no more than a small proportion of their potentiality achieved. Many are called but few are chosen, because few have the wit, application and perseverence to make the best of their possibilities.

There remain the actors who are not great, but may fairly be called 'good', who have developed a reasonable part of great potentiality; or it may be that the potential was comparatively small but the development exceptionally thorough.

Undeveloped and undisciplined talent does not last. Sooner or later the weaknesses become apparent and stand in the way of achievement. The weeds choke the flowers and prevent them coming to fruit, On the other hand, highly and conscientiously developed talent is worthless without the generosity and amplitude of character which make the artist's gift acceptable.


## Moved to the depths

It is a question often debated whether an actor should feel in performance the emotions which he is trying to express. My view is that obviously strong emotion cannot, and should not, be fully felt in performance. For one thing, it is impossible to have really deep feeling on call and to cough it up punctually between eight thirty and eleven every evening. For another thing, the physical accompaniments to deep feeling – disturbance of the diaphragm, for instance, muscular tension, uncontrollable sobs, tears and so on – prevent an actor from projecting his performance, as well as disturbing its rhythm and discipline, thereby disconcerting his colleagues, who would be compelled to react differently according as his performance varied emotionally and technically.

Of course there must be some feeling, but it must be under technical control. The 'real', or full, feeling must be experienced at some stage in the preparation of the part. It is the actor's business to experiment at rehearsal and, especially, in private, with technical ways of expressing such feeling.

The fact that an actor sheds 'real' tears in performance, like the player in *Hamlet*, must not be regarded as evidence of 'real' feeling. For many people, men as well as women, tears come easily and can be shed at will. Also, is it your experience that tears are a manifestation of deep grief? One weeps at a pathetic incident, not a tragic one. When the curtain falls on *Quality Street* or *Sweet Lavender* the hankies are dabbing at misted eyeglasses. At the end of *Oedipus Rex* the audience leaves dry-eyed.

Stanislavsky, in his important book *An Actor Prepares*, discusses how an actor may teach himself to 'feel' and how he may technically recreate such feeling and express it in the theatre. I think that his theories are, perhaps, a little cut and dried. It is assumed that a similar method may be applied to each and every actor. The so-called 'Method', recently so influential on American actors, derives very largely, and admittedly, from Stanislavsky and the Moscow Art Theatre. Twenty years ago it was being hailed by young people in New York as a great innovation. But I find it hard to believe that, with variations to suit different natures and different occasions, good actors have not been applying such a 'Method' for centuries. It consists in recalling analogous experiences to those which the character whom you are impersonating is called upon to undergo. If you have no exactly analogous experience, you think of something as nearly parallel as your own, possibly rather limited, experience permits: if you have not experienced the death of a parent, you recall the death of a beloved dog. You relive the experience as vividly as you possibly can. You 'react' to it, and you then endeavour to express the emotions which you have 'found'. That is to say it must be, as far as possible, untainted by the stereotypes of acting; the back of the hand, for instance, pressed to the forehead to express grief.

Theoretically this is fine. But have you noticed how often in 'real life' people react to events, to real events, in an almost unbelievably 'ham' way? I was a bystander once at a motor smash. I was quite uninvolved with any of the victims and therefore able to watch the goings-on with detachment. The behaviour of the spectators, no doubt including myself, could have been reproduced as a Hideous Example of Bad Acting. One person pressed the back of his hand against his forehead in token of grief or horror; another pressed his hands forward, palms outwards, as if to avert danger; I caught myself in a sort of crouching position, knees bent, uttering the deathless line, 'Oh no!'

Of course, this is not intended to be a defence of 'ham' or stereotyped acting. All I want to suggest is that the reaction against it has gone too far. Real life is full of stagey incidents and stagey behaviour, and there is no particular merit in the sort of acting which shuns staginess, unless it clearly substitutes something more interesting and moving. This is what 'method' acting rarely does. Too often it produces tiny manifestations, which appear to be symptoms of constipation rather than of any recognizable emotion. This is not because 'The Method' is wrong. It is because too often its practitioners attempt to apply amateur psycho-analysis and then to express the result with inadequate technical means. There is no great point, so it seems to me, in an actor having splendid, original and 'pure' ideas which he has never learned to express; no point in having 'know-what' unless he has adequate 'know-how'.


*Knowing what kind of play you're in*

In general, I suppose that what is considered 'good' acting is that which is convincing and also appropriate to its context. Few actors can be good in all kinds of context, be that the style of the play, the size and shape of the house or the quality of the audience.

John Gielgud once defined 'style' in acting as 'knowing what kind of play you're in'. This seems to me a splendidly comprehensive, practical and intelligent definition about which reams of pretentious rubbish have been written, mostly by learned persons with small experience of the practical realities of the stage.

Shakespeare, Sheridan, Shaw, O'Neill or Pinter, to take, almost at random, five important dramatists writing in English, all demand a different style from the actor. This is partly because the content of their plays differs very widely; partly because each is writing in a different context, whether of time, place, social situation and so on; and partly because each of these writers has a different idea of the manner in which he expects his actors to relate themselves to the audience. As a result, each employs a different style of diction. Pinter's, for instance, is the most informal and egalitarian, Sheridan's the most formal, Shaw's the most intellectual and instructive, Shakespeare's and O'Neill's the most passionate.★ There are, of course, dozens of other qualities in which these five both resemble and differ from each other. But it is clear that an actor cannot successfully impersonate their characters without quite drastic variations in both his imaginative and technical approach.

The style of the play must determine the qualities which an actor must bring to bear. For example, in a play by Chekhov subtlety and delicacy of feeling will be all-important: no extreme technical demands are made. Marlowe offers small scope for subtle nuances, but large scope for robustious declamation and physical action. Shakespeare requires both the delicate and the robustious attack, obviously not at the same moment, but often at different moments of the same performance.

A critic estimating a performance will rightly praise an actor for economy of means in such a part as Willy Loman (*Death of a Salesman*) or Joseph Surface (*School for Scandal*), whereas economy of means would be less appropriate in Lady Bracknell (*Importance of Being Earnest*) or Croaker (*Good Natured Man*). In other words, economy of means is only a virtue in an appropriate context; in another context flamboyance is a virtue. It is a question of suitability. Just as some parts demand height and dignity where others call for a squat person of vulgar deportment.

The good actor, however, is not necessarily the one who always sticks to obviously appropriate parts, who never attempts a rôle which is not well within his natural range. Personally I admire more the actor who will have a go at a part which is not quite within his compass, but who wants to expand his range by playing parts for which he is not obviously suited.

One of the frustrating things about the commercial theatre, as it exists in our modern metropolitan cities, is that it is commercially very ill-advised for a 'star' actor to venture outside the range of parts in which the public is accustomed to see him. One of the advantages of repertory theatre, in which the same company is seen in a number of different plays, is that the actors get cast in a much wider range of parts.

Gerald du Maurier, for example, was perhaps the most admired actor of the English stage for about thirty years until his death in 1954. But, although he was in a position to play any part which he wanted, he never ventured outside a range in which, year after year, he appeared looking and sounding exactly the same intelligent, sensitive, exceedingly attractive gentleman.

For years Lynn Fontanne has appeared in a series of Lynn Fontanne parts. She plays them

---

★ Shakespeare's passion differs from and exceeds that of O'Neill not necessarily in feeling, but because Shakespeare is able to clothe his feeling in magnificent vesture, an immense vocabulary (some of it self-invented), and an extraordinary musicality, which commands a range of melody and rhythm such as no other poet in the English language can approach. Shakespeare can also heighten passion by unrivalled use of pathos and humour. O'Neill's dialogue, on the other hand, is conducted in a small, dull vocabulary and when, now and again, it rises above the small change of conversational currency, it is apt to be embarrassingly purple and inflated. Nevertheless, his feeling is so powerful and sincere that again and again emotion is communicated almost in spite of, rather than by means of, the language.

Is there an analogy here with American acting? So often it seems that the actors are so unaccustomed to rhetoric, to any musicality of speech, any attempt to use language for any purpose other than to convey prosaic ideas and practical information, that they are afraid to venture outside the territory of conversational commonplace. Consequently, when passionate ideas are expressed, the actors, with no rhetorical skills at their command, are apt to be noisy and violent and their passion is apt to sound vulgar. On the other hand, where American acting is especially touching and interesting is in the groping towards passionate expression which has to remain inarticulate.

marvellously, but they do not reveal what one suspects to be an infinitely wider potentiality. Even when she elected to play in Dürrenmatt's alarming play *The Visit*, instead of presenting a picture of corruption, the same gracious, elegant, delightful lady emerged with, in my opinion, a disastrous emasculation of a powerful play.

Had either of these two actors been members of such a company as the British National Theatre or any of the top French, German or Russian repertory companies, their range would have been greatly expanded. On the other hand, it has to be admitted that their incomes would have been greatly reduced and they would almost certainly not have attained such a high degree of eminence and celebrity.

It is a dilemma which every actor of very great talent has to face and to which he is entitled to find his own solution. Do I want to make the most of my talent imaginatively and technically? Or, alternatively, do I want to use my talent in the way most popular with the public and therefore most financially profitable to me?

In case we are tempted, perhaps a little priggishly, to decide that the first is the 'right' alternative, let us remember that one of the important uses, or duties, of an actor is to give pleasure. And there can be no question that one of the chief sources of pleasure for an audience is the feeling of contact with a 'star', with a person of exceptional magnetism and wide celebrity.

## Star personality

Now, except for the very, very few actors of near-genius, of whom there are never more than three or four simultaneously extant, the only way to become a 'star' is by exploiting your 'personality', by finding aspects of yourself which have the potentiality of immense popularity, and then by stressing these over and over again, in performance after performance, until they become familiar to an immense public and an inseparable element of your public 'persona'. Physical beauty is the most obvious of such aspects, but there are others not less important: humour, wit, the ability to feel and express powerful emotion, perhaps most important of all that indefinable, widely various quality called 'charm'.

It is a fact that quite untalented actors can be greatly successful as film-stars. This fact has seriously, but maybe temporarily, cheapened the art of acting. Young people aspire not to be an actor but to be a star. The two are not the same. Of course it is not absolutely essential that a film-star be incapable of acting. Many have been splendid actors, Pauline Frederick, for instance, Nazimova or Charles Laughton. But many haven't. I doubt if anyone would claim that Greta Garbo or Gary Cooper were actors of even moderate talent. Yet their stellar attributes cannot be questioned. It is impossible to believe that such interesting and wonderful-looking creatures could possibly be ignoble or dislikable or even dull. They made their effect by 'appearing' and by 'being', not by 'acting'; and by placing themselves in the hands of expert technicians – directors, camera-men, hairdressers, tailors, producers, agents. There is no need for a film-star to learn to 'project', no need for him to think much or feel much. Thought and feeling can be inferred by the audience from the context, if the director knows his business. Nevertheless, you or I, or little Mr Hubble down the road, couldn't substitute for Gary Cooper. And a good actor couldn't either. He would probably play the rôles *much* better, but that, alas, is not quite the point.

*These three abide*

So we have, probably always have had, and always will have great actors, good actors, and – a class apart – 'Stars'.

There have always been people whom the public wanted to see. La Belle Otèro was one; Lily Langtry, the Jersey Lily, was another; the Abbé Liszt was a third. Now and again well-known boxers or bullfighters appear as stars, not fighting and really not acting either, just on display. I think people want to see them partly as splendid physical specimens, but even more just because they are celebrated. The wish to be in contact with celebrity is a strong one and almost universal. Do we imagine that, if we come within a certain distance of a famous person, some of the magic will rub off on us? Is it a feeling comparable to that which drove thousands of childless women to the home of the Dionne family in Quebec, to touch the house, to pick and take away stones from the neighbourhood, just to breathe the air, in the hope that what had made Madame Dionne produce quintuplets might somehow induce in them a magic fertility? Or is it that contact, however casual, just passing a famous person in the street, makes us feel that we are moving nearer than usual to the sources of wealth and power and inspiration?

There are 'stars' who, without beauty or notoriety, are so magnetically talented that they can draw a public to see any nonsense in which they choose to appear. Of this kind the chief example at this moment is Barbra Streisand. There are always a few artists of this calibre. It seems odd that they never manage to bring their extraordinary gifts to bear upon more important material. Perhaps their gifts are of such a kind that they only show to advantage in trivial material; or that they can only adapt whatever text they use to the service of talents so brilliant that we are all dazzled into forgetting how very limited is their range.

Where Duse, according to Shaw, was a great actress, Bernhardt was a star. She certainly seems to have had the potentialities of a great actress: a strong, creative talent – her paintings and sculpture, as well as her acting, bear witness to this – excellently produced voice, excellent diction, considerable musicality, imaginative, with simply enormous physical energy, and, finally, that amplitude and generosity of character without which no artist can be great. But she allowed her career to degenerate. Eventually she no longer sought to impersonate the characters of creative writers, but relied increasingly on 'Vehicles' in which she might lucratively impress a large international public with her 'personality'.

*Steady on, Mr Shaw!*

Bernard Shaw, in my opinion the greatest dramatic critic who has written in the English language, repeatedly names as the greatest actors of his day, Duse, Ristori, Coquelin and Salvini. He is biting about Sarah Bernhardt, whom he regarded merely as a star. His comparison of her art with that of Duse is so instructive about both acting and criticism, and incidentally, about both ladies and, especially, about the critic himself, that I shall quote it almost in full. He is writing in the London *Saturday Review*, dated 15 June 1895 in a week after Bernhardt and Duse had each appeared in her own production of Sudermann's *Magda*.

'. . . The contrast between the two Magdas is as extreme as any contrast could possibly be between artists who have finished their twenty years' apprenticeship to the same profession under closely similar conditions. Madame Bernhardt has the charm of a jolly maturity, rather spoilt and petulant, perhaps, but always ready with a sunshine-through-the-clouds smile if only she is made much of. Her dresses and diamonds, if not exactly splendid, are at least splendaceous; her figure, far too scantily upholstered in the old days, is at its best; and her complexion shows that she has not studied modern art in vain. Those charming roseate effects which French painters produce by giving flesh the pretty colour of strawberries and cream, and painting the shadows pink and crimson, are cunningly reproduced by Madame Bernhardt in the living picture. She paints her ears crimson, and allows them to peep enchantingly through a few loose braids of her auburn hair. Every dimple has its dab of pink; and her fingertips are so delicately incarnadined that you fancy they are transparent like her ears, and that the light is shining through their delicate blood-vessels. Her lips are like a newly-painted pillar-box; her cheeks, right up to the languid lashes, have the bloom and surface of a peach; she is beautiful with the beauty of her school, and entirely inhuman and incredible. But the incredibility is pardonable, because, though it is all the greatest nonsense, nobody believing in it, the actress herself least of all, it is so artful, so clever, so well-recognized as part of the business, and carried off with such a genial air, that it is impossible not to accept it with good-humour.

One feels, when the heroine bursts upon the scene, a dazzling vision of beauty, that instead of imposing on you, she adds to her own piquancy by looking you straight in the face, and saying in effect, 'Now who would ever suppose that I am a grandmother?' That, of course is irresistible; and one is not sorry to have been coaxed to relax one's notions of the dignity of art when she gets to serious business and shows how ably she does her work. The coaxing suits well with the childishly egotistical character of her acting, which is not the art of making you think more highly or feel more deeply, but the art of making you admire her, pity her, champion her, weep with her, laugh at her jokes, follow her fortunes breathlessly, and applaud her wildly at the fall of the curtain. It is the art of finding out all your weaknesses and practising on them – cajoling you, harrowing you, exciting you – on the whole fooling you. And it is always Sarah Bernhardt in her own capacity who does this to you. The dress, the title of the play, the order of the words may vary; but the woman is always the same. She does not enter into the leading character: she substitutes herself for it.'

This is a marvellous description of Star acting, as opposed to great, or even good acting. Do you agree that it is rather too cruel, too subjectively coloured by the writer's personal antipathy to Bernhardt? Are not the references to her make-up, strawberries and cream, the lips like a newly painted pillar-box . . . are not these gratuitously insulting? And is not the insistence on her jollity, good humour and so on, merely an instance of the old, old critical trick of damning with faint praise, condoning some petty fault, in order to come down the more effectively on a more important shortcoming? In this case there is more to it than that. The jollity, the prettiness, the charming coaxing ways are being stressed, so that in the next paragraph the absence of such qualities in the art of Duse may be used the better to demolish Madame Sarah.

He writes of Duse . . .

'When she comes on the stage, you are quite welcome to take your opera-glasses and count whatever lines time and care have so far traced on her. They are the credentials of her humanity; and she knows better than to obliterate that significant handwriting beneath a layer of peach-bloom from the chemists. The shadows on her face are grey, not crimson; her lips are sometimes nearly grey also, there are neither dabs nor dimples; her charm could never be imitated by a barmaid with unlimited pin-money and a row of footlights before her instead of the handles of a beer-engine.'

This is pretty shocking stuff, do you agree? Perhaps it is rather comforting that a critic so pre-eminent and a man so kind and fastidious as Bernard Shaw, should, now and then, like the rest of us, sink to cheapness and vulgarity; should, like any other dramatic critic, sink to making his column more readable by personal ribaldry at the expense of those who cannot answer back. It has on me the effect of putting me off Duse, the good child standing smugly by, while Bernhardt, the bad child, gets a good smacking. Bernhardt, one thinks, must have been pretty powerful stuff to make so great a man so mean and spiteful.

'. . . Obvious as the disparity of the two famous artists has been to many of us since we first saw Duse, I doubt whether we, any of us realized, after Madame Bernhardt's very clever performance as Magda on Monday night, that there was room in the nature of things for its annihilation within forty-eight hours by so comparatively quiet a talent as Duse's. And yet annihilation is the only word for it. Sarah was very charming, very jolly when the sun shone, very petulant when the clouds covered it, and positively angry when they wanted to take her child away from her. And she did not trouble us with any fuss about the main theme of Sudermann's play, the revolt of the modern woman against that ideal of home which exacts the sacrifice of her whole life to its care, not by her grace, and as its own sole right and refuge, but as a right which it has to the services of all females as abject slaves.

In fact there is not the slightest reason to suspect Madame Bernhardt of having discovered any such theme in the play; though Duse, with one look at Schwartze, the father, nailed it to the stage as the subject of the impending struggle before she had been five minutes on the scene. Before long, there came a stroke of acting which will probably never be forgotten by those who saw it, and which explained at once why those artifices of the dressing-table which help Madame Bernhardt would hinder Duse almost as much as a screen placed in front of her. I should explain, first, that the real name of the play is not *Magda* but *Home*. Magda is a daughter who has been turned out of doors for defying her father, one of those outrageous persons who mistake their desire to have everything their own way in the house for a sacred principle of home life. She has a hard time of it, but at last makes a success as an opera singer, though not until her lonely struggles have thrown her for sympathy on a fellow-student, who in due time goes his way, and leaves her to face motherhood as best she can. In the fullness of her fame she returns to her native town, and in an attack of home-sickness makes advances to her father, who consents to receive her again. No sooner is she installed in the house than she finds that one of the most intimate friends of the family is the father of the child. In the third act of the play she is on the stage when he is announced as a visitor. It must be admitted that Sarah Bernhardt played this scene very lightly and pleasantly: there was a genuine good fellowship in the way she reassured the embarrassed gallant and made him understand that she was not going to play off the sorrows of Gretchen on him after all these years, and that she felt she owed him the priceless experience of maternity, even if she did not particularly respect him for it. Her self-possession at this point was immense: the peach-bloom never altered by a shade. Not so with Duse. The moment she read the card handed her by the servant, you realized what it was to have to face a meeting with the man. It was interesting to watch how she got through it when he came in, and how, on the whole, she got through it pretty well. He paid his compliments and offered his flowers; they sat down; and she evidently felt that she had got it safely over and might allow herself to think at her ease, and to look at him to see how much he had altered. Then a terrible thing happened to her. She began to blush; and in another moment she was conscious of it, and the blush was slowly spreading and deepening until after a few vain efforts to avert her face or to obstruct his view of it without seeming to do so, she gave up and hid the blush in her hands. After that feat of acting I did not need to be told why Duse does not paint an inch thick. I could detect no trick in it: it seemed to me a perfectly genuine effect of the dramatic imagination.'

All this may be cruelly unfair to Bernhardt, unduly partial to Duse. It is indicative of the critic's bias that he refers throughout the article to Madame Bernhardt, Sarah Bernhardt, even Sarah; whereas the rival actress is always Duse, as it might be Beethoven, Titian, Ibsen. Why, incidentally, are Leonardo and Michelangelo, always spoken of thus instead of as Da Vinci and Buonarroti?

However, whether right or wrong about the two particular actresses, the critique does distinguish, with its author's characteristic wit, clarity and precision, the great artist from the mere Star: a more mature, less childishly selfish conception of what acting is about.

This is not to say that great actors are profound and mature all the time, any more than are great archbishops. They are, after all, human; and actors' work is done in more emotional, nerve-racking, risky and vulgarly public circumstances than attend the work of an archbishop. If an actor under the inevitable stress of his task behaves in a foolishly 'temperamental' way to a colleague, or says some indiscreet, silly thing which gets quoted in the Press, one must not therefore conclude that he is an habitually silly indiscreet fellow.

In general, the great actor, as opposed both to the Star and to the merely competent practitioner, is distinguished, not by superior physical attributes, or skill, or even energy, so much as by a greatness of spirit.

# 6 *Looking ahead*

*Changes in the theatre*

The theatre has existed for about two and a half thousand years. During that period it has, naturally, changed a great deal, not always moving onwards and upwards but at least surviving. Right now it is changing considerably. But it would be unwise to say, because they are occurring in our own lifetime and we are therefore very conscious of them, that such changes are more rapid or more drastic than ever before.

Nevertheless, rapid and drastic changes are taking place, principally caused by the fact that the 'live' theatre is no longer the principal means of the distribution of drama. Films, first, then television have technical facilities for a vastly wider and more economical distribution of drama than a 'live' theatre has ever had, or can ever have. For example, a single performance of a television play can be available to an audience of many millions, an audience which could fill a theatre nightly for ten or fifteen years; and the same performance can be taped and revived as often as desired. This means that far more money can be available for such a production. In fact, however, the money and the time which are made available are usually quite inadequate to secure a high standard of performance. But this is due not to any inherent flaw in the nature of television or film-making, but rather to the fact that, in America nearly always, and elsewhere more often than not, artistic standards are considered less important than profitability.

This is understandable. Financial profitability can be objectively determined by counting heads. Artistic standards are a matter of subjective judgement.

The exploitation first of films, then of television as money-making enterprises and, as a consequence, their subjection to what is believed to be 'popular' taste, has greatly retarded the development of significant and serious work in both media. This is not because 'popular' taste is any worse than 'mandarin' taste; it is because 'popular' taste is no less subjective; and the film moguls, in their search for what is popular and therefore money-making are just as much at a loss to establish objective standards as are artists and critics to establish objective standards of excellence. The moguls tend habitually to underestimate public taste, just as artists and critics tend to overestimate it. The result is that the moguls of film and television give the public not what it wants but what they – the moguls – subjectively believe it wants.

In fact the public doesn't know what it wants. In general it is thought safe to assume that sexual titillation will be unfailingly popular. But it is not safe to assume, as the moguls so often and disastrously do, that what titillates on Monday will still titillate on Thursday, that what was a bit of Yum-yum in Chicago will seem equally yummy in Leamington Spa. Of course no sensible mogul would think of pandering for one instant to the taste of Leamington Spa, because Chicago is such a much more important market. This still further depresses the quality of the mass-distributed article. The taste of the large market is not necessarily superior to that of the small; indeed there are good reasons why it may in many important ways be inferior. But taste is a subjective matter: moguls prefer to base decisions on objective grounds. In other words, money talks.

*How does all this affect the actor?*

All this means that the overwhelming majority of professional actors now earn the greater part of their income in films and television.

It is still true that most of the experienced leaders of the profession were trained and spent their early years in the theatre. But this generation is already being superseded by younger people, to whom 'acting' primarily means acting in films and television, under the artistic, technical and economic conditions, which they, not the theatre offer.

As we have already discussed, films and television demand of most of their actors only a very limited degree of skill. It is very usual for an actor to get a call from his agent to be at such-and-such a studio at nine the next morning. The fee will be so-and-so. There is a guaranteed minimum of three days.

'The part?'
'Oh, I didn't ask. They'll tell you when you get there.'

This kind of thing undermines pride in craftmanship. Your work is a routine task in a factory and it is not very relevant that it is a drama-factory, a dream-factory, a fun-factory rather than a soap-factory.

More important players, entrusted with more difficult and responsible parts, do need craftsmanship. Quite apart from dramatic expression, it is important and, from a crafts-man's point of view, interesting to master the techniques of addressing yourself to micro-phone and camera, to co-operate with the technicians, to appreciate the pattern which the director is trying to achieve and to fit into it; in short, to be skilful and co-operative in order to avoid wasting the company's precious time.

All this means that the modern actor's career is subservient, which was not the case fifty, even thirty years ago, to large financial and technological organizations in which his posi-tion is comparatively less important and responsible than in the theatre.

Unless he is playing a very important rôle, an actor is a much more dispensable element in the organization's product than any of six or eight technicians; camera-man, sound man, lighting expert, studio manager and so on. With the passing of the years I do not see the television and film actor regaining any of the dignity and responsibility which were diminished when he left the theatre. Naturally, this reduced responsibility and significance cannot but adversely effect his work.

*Recruits then*

Fifty years ago I would estimate that the majority of recruits to the theatre either came of a theatrical family or else joined the profession because they were stage-struck.

Children of theatrical families got their apprenticeship from a very tender age, and began with very few romantic illusions about 'The Profession'. Theatrical lodgings, theatrical land-ladies, stage-doorkeepers, were to them figures as familiar from earliest days as are their neighbours, aunts, uncles or the postman to ordinary children. Many theatrical children were veteran actors by the time they were nine years old. It does not follow, of course, that they were talented veterans, or cultivated or interesting or lively people. Most of them were not in the least dedicated artists but were simply following the line of least resistance, But they did, at a very early age, know their way about the stage.

A friend of mine, whose forebears had been professional actors for generations, recalls all the children of the family being made by their father to read aloud from the newspaper from the time that they could read at all. For a year or two before that, they had been made to recite nursery rhymes. Each child had a lesson from father every morning, while mother was out at the butcher's or the grocer's collecting provisions. For the youngest the lesson might last no more than two or three minutes, no longer than it takes to say *Little Jack Horner* three or four times. But the babies had to be present and get what profit they could, while the other kids received their more advanced instruction. All this took place in front of the fire in the parlour of the 'digs', and the bigger children had to read aloud in such a manner as to cause a wine-glass set on the chimney-piece to 'ring'. This was to ensure that the child was projecting his voice. It has always sounded to me like a splendid piece of technical education.

The stage-struck aspirant with no previous experience had to pick up the elements of his craft as he went along. My own first engagement followed an appearance in amateur theatricals at Oxford. I was then asked to join a repertory company because the director had found me 'striking and effective' in a part which had just happened to turn my many shortcomings into advantages. The first production was Shaw's *Heartbreak House*, and who was to play the leading part, a sea-captain of eighty years? Why, none other than the Wonder-boy from Oxford! I lasted until lunchtime of the first day's rehearsal. I was then taken aside and told it had all been a great mistake. I could leave that minute, not even come back after lunch, or I could stay and assist the stage-manager. Of course I stayed, but I was of no assistance to the stage-manager or anyone else. However, the stage-manager, who was called Herbert Lugg, and to whom I am for ever grateful, was kind and I was eager, if ignorant; indeed too ignorant to know how grossly ignorant I was. However, when told by Herbert to go *there* and do *that*, I *flew* there and *did* that and gradually, very gradually, began to get the hang of things.

It is still possible to make a similar beginning. But only just. All the time the opportunities get fewer. There are fewer and fewer professional companies. In the high-pressured, intensely competitive theatres of Broadway and London no one has time to waste on ignorant beginners.

*Recruits now*

How in this epoch does a would-be professional get a start? The answer should be, I suppose, in a drama school or the drama department of a university. Yet this answer has never carried great weight with those who cast plays, whether in the theatre, films or television.

Rightly or wrongly, we suspect that the products of theatrical education are apt to be full of theories derived from books. At the drop of a hat they'll start quoting Artaud at you, or Brecht or Castelvetri or even Eric Bentley. We reflect that the best actors are, in our experience, hardly ever the products of a drama school or university.

We reflect that drama schools are run by people who are good at organizing: splendid sensible, capable people, often idealistic, but not necessarily people with marked theatrical gifts or even taste.

We reflect that the drama departments in universities are run by scholars, persons who know a great deal about the theoretical aspects of their subject, but who are rarely knowledgeable about, or even interested in, the practical details of acting. The best actors I have known are hardly any of them well-educated or intellectual. They are intelligent, but not a bit scholarly. So we look for professional experience and do not inquire too deeply into an actor's education.

I said this once to a student in a mid-West college. He was a worthy young fellow, full of eagerness and idealism. He was amazed and shocked.

'You mean They (meaning potential employers) won't be interested in what sort of a degree I get?'
'Most unlikely.'
'Well!'
'I don't think the question will ever arise!'
'Then what *will* they be interested in?'

Feeling rather ashamed, I had to explain that 'straight A's' were considerably less saleable than straight legs, a good chest and an audible voice. I could not help feeling that his professors ought to have explained this already. But I really believe that they too thought that straight A's were the passport to theatrical fame and fortune.


*A great gulf fixed*

It may be that theatrical people are wrong and unjust about all this. And it certainly is a great pity and damaging to both sides, that such a wide gap separates the professional from the academic theatre. Currently 'we', on the professional side, fault the academic because, again and again, we find students stuffed to the gills with ideas and information which are, no doubt, relevant for teachers of literature, historians and so on and which are, no doubt, an enrichment to anyone, but which are almost totally irrelevant as part of the professional equipment of a beginning actor. Contrariwise, these same beginners arrive knowing almost nothing at all about important elements of their craft, notably the technique of speech.

The academics justly fault the professional theatre for its lack of serious purpose, its excessive and vulgar concentration on commercial objects, especially commercialized sex.

Furthermore, each side is jealous of the other. 'We' resent the fact that 'They' enjoy a higher degree of public respect than any but highly 'successful' artists. The public assumption is that a Professor is not only learned, but wise and good, until he conspicuously proves himself otherwise; whereas about the Actor the assumption is that he is frivolous, ignorant and unreliable, not until he proves himself otherwise, but until he himself proves 'successful' in terms of money-making and celebrity.

The academic, by virtue of his profession, is at an early stage of his career assured of 'tenure'. Tenure means that, unless he is actually caught with his fingers in the cash-box or in bed with a student, he is assured of an adequate salary for the rest of his career and a pension at the end. The actor in the English-speaking countries can, if successful, intermittently earn spectacular sums of money, swingeingly taxed, but his livelihood is never assured and no pension awaits the end of his career.

I remember being present as a member of a committee which had to decide the remuneration of the Organizer – a full-time annual appointment – of an Arts Festival in a university. The committee, apart from myself, consisted exclusively of academics. They were sincerely anxious to be just, but formidable prejudice appeared. They clearly regarded the organization of the Arts Festival as rather vulgar. Pejorative words kept cropping up, like 'Entrepreneur' and 'Impresario': visions floated in the air of astrakhan collars, champagne luncheons with actresses, or, worse, opera-singers, (females, of course; no one supposed that the baritones would get their lunch) and screams rang out when a salary was suggested which put the 'Impresario' ahead of the Assistant Professor of Geography.

Educational institutions, however, do believe that there exists a respectable aspect of theatre. This goes under the name drama, which is, of course, merely a branch of English Literature, and its connection with a professional theatre may be safely ignored. One can 'teach' drama in schools and colleges, one can even have a drama department and a university theatre without losing face, provided its staff has unimpeachable academic qualifications untainted by professional vulgarity. Money may be forthcoming for the activities of drama departments, but only if the givers can be assured that they are supporting not entertainment but education.

This attitude constitutes a most serious danger to the professional theatre and professional acting. The 'live' theatre can easily survive the comparatively simple economic and technical threats which the mass-distributive media can offer. The academic threat is more insidious, because it is well-intentioned and is not consciously intended as a threat.


*Why is this academic threat so dangerous?*

Educational institutions pay lip-service to the value of drama. It is sincerely claimed that there is something called great drama, which is an important, even indispensable, part of our cultural heritage; but it is denied that great drama must be, if not greatly, then at least highly skilfully performed.

Two instances in support of this: a few years ago I lectured (about drama) in a huge and justly celebrated American university. The audience was a very large one. I assumed, since they had come to my lecture, that they all had some interest in the subject, but asked those actually 'studying' drama to put up their hands. Five or six hundred hands shot up.

'How many have ever seen a play professionally performed?'
Maybe two hundred hands.
'How many have ever seen a classical play professionally performed?'
Six or eight hands.
'How many plan to make the theatre a career?'
Not one hand.

Afterwards I asked the professor at the head of the drama department how many of his students had graduated to professional work in the theatre. He was a learned man, also a kind and reasonable man, but he clearly thought my question absurd. He pondered it: 'In the last *twenty* years, just one.' Then, with a ferocious glitter of rimless glasses: 'A woman – thank God.' 'Then what,' I asked, 'will become of all these drama students?'
'They will teach.'
'Teach what?'

Again he looked at me as if I had two heads.

'Well, naturally, drama.'

The second instance concerns Queen's University, Belfast. Some money had been allocated to create an arts centre and it was proposed that the plan should include a theatre. The money immediately available was not enough to plan anything but a thoroughly unambitious building.

In the immediate neighbourhood of the university there exist two small theatres. One operates professionally, but unsuccessfully, because a cripplingly small budget greatly curtails standards; and the budget is conditioned by the fact that the auditorium holds only 350 people. The other theatre belongs to a teachers' training college, its capacity is also too small to make full professional use feasible; however it is handsomely and flexibly designed, primarily for use by the college, and it could be used by other suitable tenants.

It is my view that one or other of these theatres would be adequate for the University Amateur Drama Society, the French Department's annual get-up of Molière, the German Department's Schiller and the very occasional 'intimate' opera, which the Music Department might initiate.

Northern Ireland has for some years been without a professional theatre of any calibre. It is a community of three and half million people. Belfast is a city of about seven hundred and fifty thousand people, with a peripheral population of at least another half million. Amateur drama flourishes and the level of talent is exceptionally high. As in the rest of Ireland there is a strong theatrical tradition and a natural bent towards performance.

My view is that the university should not try to create a theatre on its own; but that it should put its not-quite adequate capital sum and its very great local prestige behind a joint scheme, sponsored by the Government, operating through the Arts Council (of Northern Ireland), the province's six County Councils and the Corporation of Belfast.

Such a scheme has the obvious drawback that none of the university's suggested partners will embark upon it without a great deal of pressure. This will take time and may, very possibly, never be achieved. But it is, in my opinion, the sole hope of bringing into being in Northern Ireland a theatre where professional troupes of the highest calibre can be presented. Without such professional pace-setting I see no possibility of establishing standards, either of performance or appreciation.

However, the committee has decided to advise the university to go ahead on its own and to put up yet another Little Theatre, the facilities and capacity of which will preclude professional productions, except by small companies working on very small budgets.

I could quote other instances, limited to my own experience, to the effect that academic opinion in general feels some responsibility towards drama, but none towards the maintenance of high standards of performance. Perhaps it would be fairer to say that academics tend to think that amateur performances under the direction of the academic can take adequate care of serious drama. It is not recognized that drama can only fully exist when a play is resplendently *acted*, when actors and audience together create a work of dramatic, not literary, art.

Education at present is injuring the theatre by failing to recognize this. This is partly a negative failure to put behind the professional theatre the prestige and authority which educational institutions very rightly command. But there is also a positive injury: the professional theatre is being opposed by a competing amateur theatre. Not only is this competitor backed by educational funds but by the damaging implication that it is an educational, as opposed to a commercial, a serious as opposed to a frivolous operation. The implication, of course, is not entirely true and probably not intended to be damaging.

One thing more: the previous two paragraphs make a general statement, to which, even in my own experience, there are shining exceptions. For example, the University of Minnesota, and its drama department, especially, has offered splendid co-operation to the professional Minnesota Theatre Company. Frank Whiting, the Professor of Drama, was largely responsible for the professional company's location in Minneapolis, and throughout the first decade of the company's existence he and his staff have supported it up to the hilt and have treated its members as colleagues not rivals.

## A serious professional theatre in Britain

Ironically enough, it was Shakespeare and his friends who started to operate their theatre in London as a privately-owned, commercial business, rather than continue as a group of actors supported by a noble, or royal, patron. Since then the theatre in the English-speaking communities has been almost entirely organized as a business, with artistic considerations playing second fiddle to financial. In 1941 in Great Britain, the State began, at first very tentatively but thereafter with increasing boldness and generosity, to offer financial subsidy to theatrical organizations (notably the Old Vic now absorbed into the National Theatre of Great Britain), which pursued a serious artistic policy. In 1970 the subsidies administered by the Arts Council of Great Britain, amounted to nearly eight million pounds of which over two million pounds were available to the theatre, not including opera and ballet. A chain of theatres all over the country offers serious and largely classical dramatic programmes. They play to very large audiences; it may be said that they are creating a new audience and a new attitude to theatre-going. Paradoxically, it is now the so-called 'commercial' theatre which is in difficulties and seeking public subsidy.

## A serious professional theatre in the United States

In the United States the idea of theatrical subsidy out of public funds has been slower to take root than in Europe and the amounts voted by Congress for this, though gradually increasing, are still ludicrously small. This is partly because America has a far less firmly rooted theatrical tradition – to most Americans a theatre simply implies a movie house; partly because there still exists a great deal of suspicion that public subsidy is bound to be followed by political interference; partly because the matter is bedevilled by the reluctance on the part of State Governments to relinquish control to Washington over any activity, even something so obviously piffling as drama; partly because there is still sufficient private backing to keep a 'commercial' theatre in being.

It is a fact that every year the combined receipts of so-called 'commercial' productions do not come within millions of dollars of equalling combined expenditure. But this must be offset against the fact that a 'smash-hit' occurs in the case of, maybe, one in twenty productions, and a 'smash-hit' may bring to a backer a return of several hundred per cent on his investment, plus the prestige and glamour involved. 'Angels' can still be rustled up to back the wildest, silliest theatrical adventures, but, if asked to back a serious policy with no likelihood of spectacular profits, the 'Angels' pout, spread their wings and fly away.

Talking of Angels, I cannot forebear to quote one of my rare encounters with the species. It was in Minneapolis and we met at a dinner party.

He was a wealthy, exceedingly handsome man, highly placed in an immense industrial concern. Over the brandy he started bragging of the enormous returns he was getting from a theatrical investment. Sincerely interested, I asked him the name of the play.

'We-ll, *that* I just can't remember.'

'Well, who was in it?'

'You mean actors? Jesus, I don't know any actors.'

'Who put it on?'

'Feller called Sam.'

'Why did you back it?'

'Oh, I thought it might be fun. Hell, it was only a thousand dollars, and now look-see, every week I get a check for . . .' and away we paddled into a congenial sunlit sea of dollars and cents.

Thus in America at present, while government subvention cannot be considered necessary to keep showbiz going, the serious professional theatre is in some real danger of extinction. And, in pragmatic terms, the attitude of educational theatre is justified. The professional theatre, it can justly say, seems to be preoccupied with showbiz and is incapable of keeping serious drama on its feet. Therefore we shall undertake the task. Perhaps it is foolish to regret this. Perhaps student actors and academic directors can do the job adequately. On the evidence of what I have seen they need professional help – badly. Some professors are gifted and skilful directors, but only some; and so long as appointments are made with regard predominantly, and usually solely, to academic qualification, the general standard of direction will be amateurish in the most pejorative sense of the word. Some undergraduates are brilliantly talented actors, but only some. And even the most brilliant actor cannot at the age of twenty-three bring to bear the maturity of personality and seasoned skill without which such parts as Lear, Othello, Macbeth, Brand, Borkman and a hundred others cannot be adequately cast.


*Trends and experiments*

At any epoch there is a good deal of journalism about New Trends. Journalists are always feverishly in quest of novelty – new trends, new personalities, new gods, new ways of presenting the same old ideas, be they political, theatrical, medical, sexual, even philosophical.

A few years ago John Osborne created in Jimmy Porter a brilliantly articulate portrait in an otherwise quite ordinary, realistic play. It was hailed as a masterpiece of 'newness' and some journalist dubbed Porter and his creator 'Angry Young Men'. The phrase caught on and, for a year or two, every play in which the Established Order was criticized, however mildly, was reported to be the work of an Angry Young Man. The label is now as out of date as 'Fin de siècle', 'Greenery-Yallery', 'Toff', 'Nut', or 'Flapper'.

At present there is a vogue for Artaud, a jumpy Frenchman who theorized about a Theatre of Cruelty. Peter Brook became interested and created a vogue. It is still 'in', though not so 'in' as it was last year, to be interested in a Theatre of Cruelty. It has replaced the Theatre of the Absurd, which is now rather 'out'.

'Experimental Theatre' is another journalistic label covering a multitude of ideas which appeal briefly to the very young in spirit. Most of the experiments are not sufficiently interesting to have more than a very short vogue and too often they are concerned with nothing more interesting or important than 'shocking' stuffy and conservative people.

Now and again experiments are conducted which gradually cease to be experimental and pass into the 'tradition' of the serious theatre. Indeed without such transfusions theatrical tradition soon becomes stagnant. Experiments which have become important tributaries to the traditional mainstream are those of the Duke of Saxe-Meiningen, of Antoine, Jean Copeau, Stanislavsky or Vakhtangov in the field of direction; of Appia, Gordon Craig, Bakst or Robert Edmond Jones in the field of theatrical design; of Diaghilev in the serious development of ballet. For this reason experiment is usually associated with the names of authors, directors or institutions, hardly ever with that of an actor.

Probably the most interesting and potentially influential Experimental Theatre at the present time is the Polish Group directed by Jerzy Grotowski. The American La Mama Group and Living Theatre have achieved some notable productions, but their work tries too hard to be 'exciting', is too hysterical and insufficiently based upon serious consideration.

What about Happenings? They may certainly be 'dramatic', in the same sense as a bus accident, an earthquake or fire in an orphanage. But I cannot see that such events are drama, in any strict sense of the word, since they are unplanned, uncontrollable and do not express any significantly coherent idea. And, while those concerned may behave dramatically, orphans silhouetted against the flames as they scramble down knotted sheets, a trapped orphan screaming at a window on the seventh floor – they are not 'acting'; their behaviour is not skilfully calculated to express a planned series of ideas nor is it consciously repeatable.

There are, of course, some dramatic Happenings, where events do follow a vaguely planned course but are liable to unforeseeable development. Such are bullfights or football matches: and it is true that such happenings do permit of a considerable degree of 'acting'. The Matador skilfully gratifies his public with a contrived display of physical grace and dexterity and by making the risk to his own safety appear even greater than it is. We have all seen the footballer, boxer, golfer, lawn-tennis champion, who 'plays to the gallery'. But surely these displays are not quite 'acting' so much as 'showing off', and there is a clear difference. Acting too can be no more than showing-off, when the actor puts display of his own qualities ahead of the expression of an author's ideas.

The tendency of most experimental theatres is towards a much more direct and spontaneous, and therefore non-intellectual, relation between performer and audience. The script tends to be less important and so does the skill, as opposed to the personal, emotional and sexual impact of the actor.

All this may very well mean that a professional theatre will in the next few decades have ceased to exist. The experimental theatre becomes less and less dependent upon professional skill and dedication, more and more inclined to seek a direct, emotional link between audience and players, in which drama approaches nearer and nearer to the spontaneous 'Happening' and recedes further and further from the greater rigidity and formality imposed by the ordered articulation of serious thought. Simultaneously the professional theatre seems to be committing hara-kiri by the anarchy and greed of its various trade unions, and by the conservatism and greed of most managers.

*The future?*

The whole future of acting as a serious profession and as an art is at stake. For economic and technological reasons most professional actors will continue to spend most of their time in the factory-work of making drama for mass-distribution under conditions which do not enable an actor to use either his highest skill or the full range of his creative possibilities.

Because of the stupidity and greed of professional management, and also because Education commands the large public funds and public respect which theatrical management notably lacks, Education is now in America doing the serious artistic work which the professional theatre has neglected; and is doing it less than efficiently because trained professional talent has been replaced by students and professors.

In Britain the situation is not quite analogous. Arts Council subsidy is providing an efficient supply of serious professional theatre, and – as yet – drama has taken no very firm root in the British university curriculum. But in another respect the situation in Britain is no better than in America: because of the centralization of film and television studios around London, the actor is even more orientated towards the mass-distributed drama than his American colleague. Fewer and fewer actors regard the theatre as either the economic or artistic focus of their professional lives.

When the present theatre-trained professional leaders disappear, and already they are disappearing fast, there must, I believe, be a considerable decline in both technical and artistic standards.

For reasons which keep recurring in this book, I am convinced that films and television are neither organized to encourage skilled, as opposed to marketable, actors, nor to develop in actors a serious and responsible attitude to their profession.

It may be that the leopards of mass-distributed drama will change their spots. It may be that I overestimate skill and seriousness as virtues in actors. It may be that the publicly subsidized theatres, which already exist in Great Britain and in a few years may exist in America, will sufficiently take care of the need for a serious theatre. Or it may be that university theatres will eventually recognize the need for higher standards of performance.

Right now the situation is bleak.

God helps those who help themselves. The greatest need is not for leopards to change spots, nor for manna to drop from a welfare-stately heaven, but for young actors to feel dissatisfaction with the current situation.

Will they?

Acting as a calling somewhere between factory-work and prostitution is in demand as never before. Acting as a serious profession is in grave danger of extinction. As always, the course of events will be determined not by the apathetic Many, but by the concerned, intelligent and determined Few. I feel confident that current prosperity will neither deceive nor corrupt the young actors who are also artists. Not for the first time nor the last, the Fabulous Invalid will amaze his doctors, confound the jealous cousins waiting to fall upon the inheritance, and justify the faithful and humble servants who have never given up hope of his survival.

# Index

*Figures in italics refer to illustration plates on pp. 33–64*